Items should be returned to the library from which they
were borrowed by closing time on or before the date
stamped above, unless a renewal has been granted.

 Swindon BOROUGH COUNCIL

THE FEUD

By the same author

Two Men, The Book Guild, 2000
A Family Affair, The Book Guild, 2001
Forbidden, The Book Guild, 2001

THE FEUD

Peter Rogers

The Book Guild Ltd
Sussex, England

First published in Great Britain in 2002 by
The Book Guild Ltd
25 High Street
Lewes, East Sussex
BN7 2LU

Typesetting in New Baskerville by
IML Typographers, Birkenhead, Merseyside

Printed in Great Britain by
Antony Rowe Ltd, Chippenham, Wiltshire

A catalogue record for this book is available from
The British Library.

ISBN 1 85776 660 1

The Ashleys and the Drummonds had been enemies for at least a hundred years. Before that they had intermarried happily until the tragedy occurred that was to set them at each other's throats. The world was going round happily and brilliantly. A Drummond was marrying an Ashley at Ashley Castle in Sussex. The groom was the handsome young Andrew Drummond and the bride was the beautiful Carla Ashley. The Drummonds had travelled from Drummond Castle in the neighbouring county of Kent for the occasion and there was jubilation for miles around with bonfires, fireworks, dancing, banquets, balls, carnivals and all kinds of entertainment.

And then came what was to be, for the married couple, the fateful honeymoon. On the first night of their married bliss Andrew strangled his wife. The shock and horror of the event divided the two families and began the feud which existed even into the eighteenth century. Duels were fought between the male members at the slightest provocation and swordsmanship was the practice of the day. Down the years the feud had been fed by enmity in an effort to avenge the death of the beautiful Carla Ashley. Andrew, the guilty bridegroom, was found hanging in the bedroom on the same night as the murder, no doubt in a fit of remorse, but his death did not serve as sufficient recompense for the Ashley family.

There was never any explanation for Andrew Drummond's behaviour. The two had loved each other deeply, as both families were only too aware. So what had happened? Was it a murder of passion? Was it a murder at all? Was it an unfortunate accident due to some indulgence

1

between the two lovers, some sexual aberration that had got out of control?

Since the tragedy there had been no intermarrying between the Drummonds and the Ashleys for fear that the tragedy might repeat itself. By the time of the present conflict there was only Lord Drummond and his young son, Andrew, to represent one family and Lord and Lady Ashley with their two children, Carl and Eloise, to represent the other.

Lord Drummond was a peace-loving man of the country, whereas Lord Ashley was an unpredictable character, somewhat eccentric and of doubtful integrity. He was an inveterate gambler and womaniser. He treated his beautiful wife abominably, ignored his daughter, Eloise, but worshipped Carl who was really a girl named Carla whom he insisted on being brought up as a boy so as to make sure that no member of the Drummond family could ever have designs on her. It was a secret known only to the girl's mother, who wholeheartedly disapproved of the ruse, and the child's nursemaid, who was sworn to secrecy at her own peril. Even Eloise, Carla's sister, was not privy to the deception. She had a nursemaid of her own and could only guess and listen to the idle gossip of the servants. She always behaved as if her sister, Little Carl as she called him, was a boy.

The family feud would no doubt have continued had not the two protagonists found themselves standing side by side at one of the levees at Windsor Castle. Normally they would have made sure that they were nowhere near each other, but owing to their both being late for the event, there was no avoiding the close contact, a contact that amused the king himself as he moved along the line of his courtiers.

'I didn't expect to see you two standing together,' he remarked. 'I thought you were daggers drawn still.'

With that he continued on his way leaving the two men to smile sheepishly at each other in their embarrassment. It was Lord Ashley who broke the spell.

'It does seem a rather ancient grudge, doesn't it?' he said.

'At least a hundred years old,' admitted Lord Drummond.

'What about burying the hatchet?' suggested Lord Ashley.

'In whose head?' asked Lord Drummond.

They both laughed. Although laughter was considered bad manners at Court, even the king turned at the sound, so unusual an occurrence was it between the two men. The king smiled to himself as he continued with his duty.

Lord Ashley was so carried away by the breach in the long standing enmity that at the end of the levee, when they were all taking refreshment, he suggested to Lord Drummond that they should hold a Reconciliation Ball at Ashley Castle, at which Lord Drummond and his son, Andrew, would be the guests of honour. Unsuspecting and trustful as he was, Lord Drummond could not but agree.

Very soon the gossip in society was that the Drummonds and the Ashleys had ended their feud and were to be reconciled. The date had been fixed for the ball at Ashley Castle and so it came about that one day Lord Drummond and Andrew found themselves starting out at dawn with their servant, Benson, driving the coach on their way from Drummond Castle.

Lord Drummond was by now a middle-aged widower. His son was twelve and often left in the care of the major-domo, Benson.

It was a great old coach in which they were travelling. It was packed with luggage and drawn by two strong horses. They were on their way to what Lord Drummond told the boy was a Reconciliation Party at Ashley Castle. The boy, Andrew, could remember in what abhorrence the name of Ashley had been held in the Drummond household. The feud, he knew, had started many years ago when a Drummond youth was accused of murdering an Ashley girl on their wedding night. So he had been told. Since that time, long before Andrew himself was born, an event that resulted in the death of his beautiful and well beloved mother, social intercourse between the two families had been forbidden or likely to end in a duel with swords or pistols. Several members of each family had already died as a result of such duelling.

It was hot in the heavy coach. The gold cushions were cool

3

to Andrew's cheek as he attempted to make himself comfortable. His father, sitting opposite, was upright and pensive, staring straight ahead, not even looking out of the window. He wore a buttoned-up blue frock coat which must have made him hot, but he was a man who never forgot his military training and so submitted to such discomfort willingly. He was obviously anxious about the forthcoming meeting of the rival families. It was all very well for the two heads of the families wanting a reconciliation, but some of the junior members might not approve. What about the Ashleys of Andrew's age?

Andrew himself wondered about the younger element of the Ashley clan. After his mother's death his father and Benson, the loyal servant, had brought him up between them. Benson, a tough, almost ugly gentleman had served in his father's regiment. He would willingly have laid down his life for Lord Drummond and his son. Apart from the female servants at Castle Drummond, Andrew had had no experience of the opposite sex, but it wasn't something he noticed. His nanny had been Benson.

Lord Drummond always looked as if he still missed his wife. Benson often told the boy how beautiful she was. When he put him to bed or helped him to dress, he would tell Andrew that when she died, his father had nearly committed suicide. The boy found it difficult to imagine such a strong, upright character as his father contemplating suicide. Evidently, however, but for the unusual relationship between master and servant, it would have actually happened. Ever since that day in the library at Castle Drummond when Benson had wrestled the pistol from his master, their already solid friendship had been further cemented.

On the halfway overnight stop before Ashley Castle, the hotel proprietor received Andrew and Lord Drummond in person. The luggage was carefully removed and they were led by their host to a suite of rooms on the first floor.

While Andrew's father was writing letters in the sitting room Andrew went out onto the balcony of his bedroom and looked over into the courtyard. Benson came to join him after feeding and stabling the horses. They saw a very smart carriage drive into the courtyard and an equally smart gentleman alight and make his way into the hotel. Before going inside he looked up at the balcony, saw Andrew and stopped. Andrew stared down at the man in fright. He didn't know who he was, but he instinctively disliked him. Judging by the look of the fancy gentleman, the feeling was mutual.

'Who was that?' Andrew asked.

'No idea,' said Benson as he stood beside him.

No more was thought about the incident until Andrew heard his father calling him. He ran into the sitting room but stopped abruptly at the open door, for standing beside his father was the man he'd just seen getting out of the carriage in the courtyard.

'Come here, Andrew,' said Lord Drummond.

Andrew walked nervously towards his father.

'I want you to meet Lord Ashley,' he said.

So the man Andrew was instinctively afraid of, the man who had looked up at the balcony as if he could kill him, was the man whose castle they were on their way to visit. Andrew couldn't help feeling that something was wrong, that something unpleasant was about to happen. This brief reverie was interrupted by his father.

'Lord Ashley has kindly come to speed us on our way to his family home,' explained Lord Drummond.

'How do you do, sir,' said Andrew, dutifully.

'Hello, Andrew,' greeted the great man with a charming smile.

Did he know who he was when he had looked up at the balcony, Andrew wondered? Perhaps he always looked at young people in that way, especially if they happened to be looking down at him from a balcony. Andrew couldn't help feeling that Lord Ashley considered himself to be at some disadvantage, as if he had been spied upon, as if his secret, whatever it was, had been discovered.

'That's all,' said his father, dismissing the boy.

Without even looking at Lord Ashley again, Andrew turned on his heel and left the room, as if expecting a knife in his back, such was his fear. Instead, he heard the two men laughing. So the reconciliation had started, he thought.

Benson was still on the balcony admiring Lord Ashley's carriage. It still stood in the courtyard, the driver making much of the two black horses. They would be black, wouldn't they, thought Andrew. The Drummond horses were grey.

'Do you know who that was, Benson?' Andrew asked, as he joined the man on the balcony. 'Lord Ashley.'

'Oh, Lord!' cried Benson, involuntarily.

'Why do you say that?' asked Andrew.

Benson was suddenly confused.

'No reason,' he replied, walking back into the room. But Andrew had never seen the man so discomfited before.

Andrew knew that Benson would never tell him the cause of his concern. He began to worry for his father, not himself. His father thought he was on his way to an important reconciliation event but was he actually walking into a trap, the slaughter of the Drummonds by the Ashleys? After all, he and his father were the only Drummonds left whereas there were plenty of Ashleys. Andrew decided that he was letting his imagination run away with him and dismissed worry from his mind.

Early next morning they set off on the last lap of the journey to Ashley Castle.

'It seems Lord Ashley travelled a long way to meet us,' Andrew said.

'He couldn't wait to reassure me,' said Lord Drummond, contentedly. 'The whole family are waiting to greet us.'

Later Lord Drummond mused: 'To come all that way to tell me, to make sure I was on my way. That man's a gentleman.' Then he said, 'Wouldn't you say so, Andrew?'

'Yes, Father,' replied Andrew, keeping his thoughts to himself. He wouldn't tell his father how Benson felt about the gentleman, or that for some unknown reason, he himself was fearful of meeting the Ashley family.

The last part of the journey took them through a dense forest. There were so many giant fir trees growing so close together that the sun could hardly seep through. The wheels of the carriage made hardly any sound as they travelled over the deep carpet of pine needles. Andrew could hear the silence of the forest with, occasionally, the wind, like the rustling of a lady's skirt, sighing across the treetops. He heard a fox bark and then the sound of a hunting horn, country sounds that he was used to enough but which disturbed his peace of mind as he imagined some poor animal being hunted by fat men on horses. Such thoughts he would never voice to his father.

It was late in the afternoon when they saw the battlements of Ashley Castle looming in the distance. To Andrew they looked menacing but Lord Drummond welcomed the sight and leaned forward eagerly in his seat to look out of the carriage window. The gates of the vast walled park surrounding the castle were opened for them by uniformed servants, the uniform almost military in appearance, but the men were obviously estate workers and not part of a private army. As they travelled up the long drive that must have been over a mile long, they could see deer browsing in the sunshine.

Apart from his persistent feeling of dread, Andrew could only wonder at the enchantment of the surroundings and at the strange sensation that he had been there before which, of course, was quite impossible. The feeling was not without precedent, though. Who has not experienced that mysterious impression when turning a corner to find that the scene is somehow familiar although it has never been seen before? For a moment Andrew's fear left him and he felt happy. Until the carriage turned a corner in the drive and he felt as if he had suddenly received a blow in the face.

Ashley Castle was grim and forbidding. Wide steps led to massive oak doors which at the moment were open because, as the carriage came to a halt, Lord Ashley and his wife came down the steps to greet them.

Lord Ashley was full of charm and goodwill as he had been at the hotel. He slapped Lord Drummond on the back with all the enthusiasm of a boisterous schoolboy. You would never think that he ever had an evil thought in his head. Yet, until recently, he had harboured a hatred of the Drummond family. Lady Ashley, too, must have shared that hatred and here she was, darkly beautiful, graceful, elegant. She greeted Lord Drummond with a kiss on each cheek. Then she turned to Andrew and seemed to be taken aback as if she had seen a ghost. She recovered quickly and bestowed similar kisses which embarrassed him, though he had to admit that she smelt nice.

They were ushered into the Great Hall of the castle where several other guests were assembled, members of the Ashley family who had been summoned to take part in the reconciliation. There was to be a grand ball in the evening to which the whole of the surrounding neighbourhood had been invited, but for the moment introductions to the family were being effected by Lord Ashley as he enumerated various cousins, aunts and uncles. He laughed as he concluded that the Drummonds were outnumbered. As they were, of course. There were only Lord Drummond and his son, and there would be no more until Andrew married or Lord Drummond remarried, which was most unlikely. Lord Drummond had no living brothers or sisters.

Among so many guests Andrew felt alone and shy and was standing a little apart from his father when a young girl came skipping towards him. She came from the back of the group and cast a ray of sunshine into the dark and gloomy hall. She wore a blue scarf, a white dress, frilled pantalettes and shoes with crossed straps over her tiny insteps. In spite of his taking in such details of her attire a flood of bashfulness overwhelmed Andrew.

'My name is Eloise,' she announced.

'I'm Andrew,' he said.

'I know,' she cried and twisted round for his benefit. 'Do you like my dress?' she asked.

'It's very nice,' replied Andrew, wondering what else he should say.

'Very nice,' Eloise echoed, imperiously. 'Is that all you can say? You should have said I look ravishing.'

'Oh.'

'Say it,' she commanded.

'You look ravishing,' Andrew repeated.

Eloise laughed attractively. 'That's better,' she said.

Despite her manner and conversation there was nothing objectionable about the girl. At twelve years of age she was brimming over with the love of life and it was infectious. She was innocence itself.

'Come with me, Andrew,' she said, taking his hand. 'I will introduce you to my mother.'

She led him among the throng of guests to none other than Lady Ashley, whom he had already met.

'Mummy,' she cried. 'This is Andrew. I'm going to call him Handy Andy.'

Andrew bowed before the beautiful lady. He stammered some kind of greeting. He couldn't remember what he said, he was so stricken by the sight of her, the love of a child for a beautiful woman. How absurd it sounded, but at the time; his feeling was very real and not all that rare. He had hardly noticed her when Lord Ashley had introduced her to him on their arrival, but he had been disconcerted by her kiss.

'Yes, dear, we've met,' said Lady Ashley, dismissively. 'Why don't you two go away and play?'

Eloise took Andrew's hand and led him out of the hall.

Andrew found himself in a picture gallery, a long, narrow corridor that seemed to join two parts of the castle together. Portraits of dead and gone Ashleys stared down at him from the walls. They were huge, full-length, lifelike portraits. There were men in armour, men dressed for the chase, ladies whose beauty wore the veil of centuries. Suddenly he and Eloise came upon a portrait that struck him with terror. He grabbed Eloise's arm.

'What is it?' she asked in alarm.

Again Andrew had the feeling that he had experienced in the carriage, the feeling that he had been here before.

The picture he was staring at was of a girl in the clothing of many years ago, but out of that past came a mysterious terror that filled his soul. It was but a fleeting moment of terror before life became commonplace once more. It was but a painting after all and the young girl beside him was warm and charming and real.

'Who is that?' Andrew asked calmly.

'That is a picture of cousin Carla,' explained Eloise. 'She looks just like my brother, little Carl.'

'Like your brother? But it's a girl,' protested Andrew.

'You'll see,' said Eloise, enigmatically.

They moved on and came to another portrait that worried Andrew.

'Who is that?' he asked.

'That is Andrew,' Eloise explained. 'A distant relation of yours.'

'Of mine?'

'Yes. He and Carla, the one you've just seen, loved each other many years ago but he murdered her on their wedding night.'

'So they're the ones,' mused Andrew.

'Yes. They're the ones.'

'What is he doing here then if he . . . ?' Andrew ventured.

'He was part of the family.'

'What happened to him?'

'He killed himself when he realised what he had done.'

'How do you know all this, Eloise?' Andrew asked.

'It's family history. We all know it. That's why we have always hated you.'

'Hated? Why?'

'Look closely,' commanded the girl. 'Who does Andrew look like?'

Andrew studied the portrait as Eloise suggested. Then a fear really did grip him. He turned to Eloise in wonder.

'It is you, isn't it?' she prompted.

'It could be, I suppose,' Andrew admitted. 'There's a certain likeness.'

'You and Carla,' Eloise explained, pointing from one portrait to the other. 'That's what the feud was all about. You murdered her and then killed yourself.'

'But that was so long ago, ages ago, long before you or I were born, Eloise.'

'I know,' Eloise said and laughed. 'It will all be forgotten now. They'll dance themselves silly tonight and the feud will be over.'

Andrew lingered by the portrait of his own likeness.

'Why don't they take his portrait down?.' he asked.

'I told you. He was part of the family.'

'Are you here?'

'Not yet. I'm not old enough. Neither is little Carl.'

'Carl?' queried Andrew, becoming confused.

'My brother.'

'Oh, yes. Where's he?'

'You'll meet him,' promised Eloise. 'He wasn't very well this morning. He stayed in bed.'

'Is he delicate?'

'As delicate as a girl,' exclaimed Eloise suddenly and ran away down the picture gallery laughing.

Andrew followed, still somewhat bewildered.

Neither Andrew nor Eloise nor Carl, whom he had not yet met, were allowed to stay up for the dancing and the festivities. Andrew's bedroom was a small room connected to his father's, and Benson helped Andrew retire as usual, arranging his clothes and making sure that he was comfortable.

'I wish we were home, Benson,' he moaned. 'I don't like it here.'

'You do as you're told, young man and go to sleep,' admonished Benson. 'This is your father's day.'

Although Andrew was extremely tired he only slept fitfully. He could hear the music in the ballroom below. Waves of laughter wafted up to him. Once he heard voices close at hand. He didn't open his eyes fully but peered through slightly opened lids. Two or three people were standing in the doorway. Lord Drummond was standing there with Lord and Lady Ashley.

'It could be him, couldn't it?' whispered Lord Ashley. 'How old is he?'

'Twelve,' said Lord Drummond.

'How can someone come back after a hundred years?' asked Lady Ashley.

11

'They can't,' said Lord Drummond. 'In any case we're supposed to have forgotten all that. That's why we're here.'

'Quite right,' echoed Lady Ashley.

'Eloise said he recognised himself,' Lord Ashley persisted.

'Well, there's bound to be a likeness down the ages, isn't there?' admitted Lord Drummond. 'I'm quite sure I look like my forebears.

'What about Carla?' asked Lord Ashley. 'Did he recognise her?'

'No,' put in Lady Ashley. 'How could he? He never knew her.'

'Are you going to let them meet?' asked Lord Drummond.

'Well, I . . .' Lord Ashley hesitated.

'Yes,' interrupted Lady Ashley, abruptly. 'Tomorrow.'

The three figures moved away after that and Andrew wondered who it was he was about to meet. The only person he hadn't met so far was Eloise's brother Carl. Is that who he was expected to meet tomorrow? A boy of his own age. It could only be Carl. He noticed that Lord Ashley was inclined to hesitate and that it was Lady Ashley who made the decision. The Ashleys and the Drummonds were now friends, so why the hesitation? Andrew was reminded of his first reaction to seeing Lord Ashley and it worried him. There was something less than straightforward about Lord Ashley, he decided.

It happened in the morning at breakfast. The young ones ate in a separate room from the grown-ups. Eloise and Andrew were tucking in happily when the door opened and the most beautiful boy in a smart sailor suit came in. He really was remarkably good looking with long eyelashes, a small, round face with a perfect mouth and lips and black hair cut short with a fringe over the gently curved forehead. He was about Andrew's age.

The boy stood hesitantly just inside the door. Then a look of fear came into his eyes as he saw Andrew and he turned to go.

'Don't go, Carl,' cried Eloise. 'This is Andrew. I call him Handy Andy.'

12

She got up and led the boy into the room, holding his hand.

Andrew got up from the table and held out his hand to shake the boy's, but the gesture was ignored. Carl sat at the table without a word. Andrew sat down again feeling rather foolish.

'Don't mind Carl,' said Eloise. 'He's in one of his moods.'

Studying the boy, Andrew could not help seeing a resemblance between him and the portrait of Carla the girl in the picture gallery, the girl whom his own ancestral double was supposed to have murdered. It struck him as strange that the participants of a tragedy that happened over a hundred years ago should now come face to face as innocent children. But Carl and Andrew were children of a similar age and the past had nothing to do with them.

Then why did Carl want to run away? Did he recognise the murderous Andrew in the present Andrew?

Benson had told Andrew when he woke him and helped him dress that the Reconciliation Ball had been a great success with a good deal of backslapping and all enmity forgotten. He couldn't understand why it hadn't happened before and thought the whole idea of the feud rather silly. Andrew wanted to agree with him, but he wasn't comfortable in Ashley Castle and didn't know why.

After breakfast the three young ones went into the garden to play, but Eloise had lost something of her exuberance. She realised that the family visit would come to an end soon and she didn't want it to. She turned suddenly to Andrew.

'I don't want you to go, Handy Andy,' she cried, tearfully.

'Don't be silly, Eloise,' said Carl. 'Of course he has to go. He can't stay here forever.'

'I don't want to lose my Handy Andy,' cried Eloise, now quite tearful, throwing her arms round Andrew's waist.

Andrew laughed and released himself and looked in an embarrassed way at Carl, who looked furious.

'Behave yourself, Eloise,' Carl said, sternly.

In their embarrassment the three of them ran laughing

down to the lake. At the same time a group of ladies, led by Lady Ashley, came out onto the terrace to admire the view. They were astonished to hear sudden screams coming from the lake as Carl, dripping wet, ran back to the terrace, found his mother and clung to her in spite of his wetness.

'He tried to drown me,' he cried, tearfully.

'Who did?' asked Lady Ashley.

'He did,' said Carl, pointing to Andrew who, with Eloise, had followed him up to the terrace.

'Did you try to drown Carl?' Lady Ashley asked Andrew.

Before Andrew had time to answer Eloise spoke up. 'Oh, Carl,' she said. 'How can you say such a thing?' She turned to her mother. 'I saw the whole thing,' she went on. 'They were both trying to balance on a log in the water. Andrew kept his balance but Carl fell in.'

'Is that true?' Lady Ashley asked Carl. 'No,' said Carl. 'He pushed me.'

'I assure you I did not,' asserted Andrew. 'We were flailing our arms about trying to keep our balance. I never touched him.'

'History repeating itself,' muttered a woman close to Lady Ashley.

Lady Ashley ignored the remark and turned to a footman.

'Take him in and dry him off,' she commanded and the sobbing Carl was led by the hand into the castle by the uniformed footman.

Eloise led Andrew into the castle away from the ladies. She held his hand and whispered, 'Don't worry about Carl. He's like a silly girl.'

In spite of the spirited company of Eloise, Andrew found the rest of the day rather dreary. Carl was obviously not anxious for his company though Andrew was strangely attracted to the boy. He would have liked to have been friendly with him and have talked to him, but for some unknown reason Carl was frightened of him. When Andrew voiced his thoughts to Eloise, she said that the boy had been made so conscious of the tragedy that had started the family feud that he almost went in fear for his life.

'But that was ages ago and the couple were married,' protested Andrew.

'Still,' concluded Eloise, 'Carl looks like Carla and you look like Andrew. It's bound to frighten him.'

Andrew had to accept that Carl was suffering from some kind of fixation, possibly nurtured over the years by his parents, and it would take a long time to break it. He wanted to talk to his father, but he was closeted most of the time with Lord and Lady Ashley or else he was out shooting with his lordship. He longed to be at home at Drummond Castle. He was unhappy with the people at Ashley Castle. Apart from Lady Ashley and her daughter, Eloise, he knew nobody and nobody wanted to know him. He did not see his father until late in the afternoon. Lord Drummond had been under the impression that Andrew, Carl and Eloise had been amusing themselves in the castle grounds in spite of the con-tretemps of the morning by the lake. He did not know that Carl had been put to bed in case his ducking had given him a chill.

'What do you think of it all, Andrew?' asked Lord Drum-mond.

'I'd rather be home,' replied Andrew.

'Don't you like the people here?'

'I like Lady Ashley.'

'She's very beautiful. What about Carl and Eloise?'

'I get on with Eloise all right. But she's a girl. I can't get on with Carl. He seems to be frightened of me.'

'He'll get used to us in time.'

'When can we go home, Father?'

'Soon.'

Andrew learned more about Carl that night when Benson put him to bed. Benson told him that Carl was in fact a girl but was being brought up as a boy to avoid the repetition of the tragedy that happened a hundred years ago.

'It's all Lord Ashley's idea, I'm told,' concluded Benson. 'Lady Ashley doesn't approve.'

'That's what you hear from the servants, is it?' asked Andrew.

15

'That's what they told me, yes,' admitted Benson, folding the boy's clothes.

'I shouldn't think it's true for one moment,' said Andrew. 'That tragedy was a long time ago.

'Oh, I know,' said Benson. 'It started the feud.'

'But that's all over now. That's why we're here,' declared Andrew, hoping that what he said was true.

Andrew thought no more about it. He dreamt that night that he and Carl were wandering in the forest, but Carl was dressed exactly as Eloise had been when he first met her. When he woke up he didn't know whether Carl was a girl or Eloise a boy. He dismissed it all as a confused dream, a fusion of what Benson had told him and what had actually happened by the lake.

Andrew naturally thought that Carl was his enemy but that was disproved the following evening.

After the reckless excitement of the Reconciliation Ball, Lord Ashley decided to retain the musicians for a musical evening. Scarcely had Benson left Andrew's bedroom after tucking him in and telling him to go to sleep than the faint sound of music came stealing up from below. Andrew sat up in bed and listened.

The temptation was too much. Music had always been a passion with him. It could make him cry. It was more than a mortal child could stand. He had to be there and watch as well as listen. He got out of bed and made for the door. He had opened it when the thought struck him that Benson would be coming back to make sure that he was all right and fast asleep. It was a habit of his, inspired by Lord Drummond, Benson being the one who virtually brought the boy up and was still bringing him up. Andrew went back to the bed and put the pillows under the bed clothes to make it look as if he was still tucked up inside. Then he crept out of the room and made his way to the landing where he could see the musicians through the banisters.

The musicians, four of them, were sitting on little gilt chairs on a dais at the end of the long drawing room. The music that they were playing made Andrew think of daffodils

16

dancing in the wind, a skylark singing high in the sky. As they were playing, the violinist looked up and saw Andrew. The man knew that the boy should be in bed, so he made no sign of having seen him, yet there was somehow an exchange of feelings. As the violinist turned his concentration to the music once more Andrew felt that there was someone beside him. He turned to see Carl and Eloise peering through the banisters with him. Andrew felt somewhat apprehensive following the previous encounter, but Carl turned and gave Andrew such a beautiful smile that Andrew could have put his arms round him and kissed him, such was the turmoil of emotion that Carl could evoke. Carl was enjoying the music as much as Andrew was. Carl reached out a hand to Andrew as he knelt beside him. As Andrew took it, Carl squeezed Andrew's hand with all his strength, grimacing happily as he did so. Andrew could not but notice what a soft, small hand it was and what little strength there was in the grip. He suddenly felt both love and pity for the boy.

When there was an interval in the concert and the servants began serving coffee and sweetmeats to the assembled guests Carl, Andrew and Eloise got up from their knees and, with suppressed giggles, scampered back to their rooms.

Andrew had never felt so happy and all thoughts of returning home suddenly evaporated.

That night he fell happily asleep thinking of Carl and what friends they could be. It was not part of the dream that he suddenly felt himself unable to breathe. He was suffocating. He tried to struggle but couldn't. Then he realised that he was awake and someone was on his bed holding a pillow over his face and pressing hard. He tried to cry out but couldn't. His nose was crumpled flat and he began to lose consciousness. In his struggle Andrew knocked something off the bedside table and the noise alerted Benson.

Suddenly the pillow over Andrew's face was flying away like a feather in the wind and the body that was crushing him went with it. He heard a dull thud as a body hit the floor beside the bed. Andrew stood up in the bed, shrieking in a kind of hysteria. He looked down and saw Benson holding Lord Ashley face down on the floor.

Andrew's shrieks brought others hurrying to his bedroom, among them his father and Lady Ashley. Lord Drummond took his son in his arms at once and tried to pacify him. The boy was shaking violently and felt cold.

'What's going on?' Lord Drummond asked, sharply.

Benson pulled Lord Ashley to his feet but still kept a firm grip on him.

'I found this man trying to smother your son with a pillow,' explained Benson.

'I had to do it,' muttered Lord Ashley. 'He would have killed my Carl.'

'Are you mad?' exclaimed Lady Ashley, in horror.

'What is this, Ashley?' demanded Lord Drummond. 'Assassination at Ashley Castle?'

'It's the boy's fault,' protested Lord Ashley. 'He's a little liar. He tried to drown Carl.'

Without another word Lord Drummond, with Andrew still in his arms, strode across the room and slapped Lord Ashley in the face with the back of his hand, causing his nose to bleed. Lady Ashley took her husband's arm and led him out of the room.

'Get dressed,' commanded Lord Drummond. 'Get him dressed, Benson. We're leaving. Get everything packed and bring the carriage round.'

'Yes, m'lord.'

Lord Drummond went out of the room and Andrew and Benson between them began to pack up their belongings.

'What's it all about, Benson?' asked Andrew.

'That man tried to kill you,' said Benson.

'But why?'

'If you ask me, the feud is not over by any means.

'But that's why we came here,' insisted Andrew. 'To end it all.'

'I know,' admitted Benson. 'It smells like a trap to me.'

'A trap? I wondered about that on the way here.'

'Oh, stop prattling and get yourself ready to leave.'

Andrew could not rid himself of his disappointment in having to leave, something that only a matter of hours ago he would have welcomed. He remembered the happy, laughing moments with the mercurial Eloise and that wonderful moment with Carl on the landing, holding hands and smiling. Where were they now, the two of them? Would he be able to say goodbye? Lord Ashley had obviously fed on the family feud until it had become an obsession with him. He was convinced that Andrew meant his precious Carl some harm, an echo of the earlier tragedy. But that was between a boy and a girl, not two boys.

Below his bedroom window Andrew could hear the trampling of the hooves of horses and the grating sound of carriage wheels on gravel. Later, down in the hall, he was standing on his own near the door. Lord Drummond and Benson stood together in earnest conversation. Apart from them Lord Ashley and someone Andrew hadn't seen before were also in earnest conversation. They were looking down on the ground as they spoke, as if in profound thought.

The main doors were opened by two footmen and Andrew noticed that two carriages were drawn up outside. One was theirs, the other was Lord Ashley's, the one that Andrew had seen driving into the courtyard at the hotel only a few days ago.

It was a clear, windy night, and about a dozen men with torches blazing and blowing in the wind gave light. Whilst Benson loaded their luggage into the carriage Lord Drummond bowed to Lord Ashley and left the castle. Lord Ashley followed, and Andrew noticed that the unknown gentleman with him held under his arm a bundle done up in a cloak from which protruded two sword hilts.

Both carriages pulled away from the castle, the running torch-men both leading and following behind.

'Aren't we going home, Father?' Andrew asked, nestling as close to him as he could.

'Eventually,' answered Lord Drummond, putting an arm round the boy who he knew must have been tired, because it was still the middle of the night.

19

'Why are all these men with torches running with us?' Andrew asked.

'You'll see.'

Lord Drummond had become stiff and formal, and Andrew wondered what was happening, for once they had passed the lodge gates at the end of the drive, he noticed that the other carriage was still with them. This puzzled him even more. They were taking the forest road and mixed with the sound of hoof beats and carriage wheels could be heard the footpads of the running torch-men.

They came to a clearing in the forest and the carriage came to a stop. They waited for a moment until the sound behind told them that the other carriage had also stopped. Everyone now alighted.

'Come with me, Andrew,' said Lord Drummond. 'And you, Benson.'

Andrew was suddenly half sick and faint with fear. He held his father's hand tightly and remembered thinking how strong and warm he was. What was about to happen he could only guess, but he was aware that the Shadow of Death was hovering near at hand.

They had not gone a hundred yards when they came to a clearing amidst the trees, a breezy, open space that the moon lit over the towering pine trees. Here the torch-men divided themselves into two lines, five yards or so apart, and stood motionless like soldiers on parade.

Lord Ashley, with his arms folded, stood with his back to Lord Drummond and Andrew. He was looking up at the clouds racing across the face of the moon. Two unknown gentlemen, drawing aside from the group, began to undo the swords from the bundle.

'Andrew,' said Lord Drummond, 'I committed a crime when I struck Lord Ashley in his own home.'

'But he tried to kill me, Father,' protested Andrew.

'For that reason also I must fight him in a duel. You understand?'

'Yes, Father,' said Andrew obediently. Then he added, 'Will you kill him?'

'I hope so.'

'So do I.'

Lord Drummond bent down, hugged his son and strode out into the torch light.

Lord Drummond and Lord Ashley took their swords and then returned them to their seconds. The swords were then bent to prove the steel measured properly and were returned to the duellists. The torch-men moved shoulder to shoulder and in the space between the two lines of torches Lord Drummond and Lord Ashley took their stand. There was dead silence for a moment, in the distance a fox barked. Andrew could hear the wind in the pines and the guttering of the torches. He could also hear his own heart thumping as Benson held his hand.

One of the unknown gentlemen called out a command and instantly came the scraping noise of the rapiers. The two combatants were perfect swordsmen. The light from the torches made the rapiers visible one minute and not the next. At first someone might have thought that the two men were playing until their fury broke loose. It was a duel to the death and both men knew it. Andrew's soul was on fire, agony in his heart as he watched. What would happen if his father were killed?

Then it happened in a flash. Lord Ashley's sword flew out of his hand, he flung his arms out as if crucified and fell to the ground in a heap. Lord Drummond's rapier had passed through his heart. He stood back.

Andrew wanted to race to his father but Benson held him back. Nevertheless he broke away from him and ran and clung to his father, who did not seem to notice his presence. Lord Drummond stood looking down at his opponent. One of the gentlemen who had accompanied Lord Ashley was on one knee supporting him in his arms. Lord Ashley's face was clay-coloured, his head drooped forward and his jaw hung loose. He tried to speak but his words were unclear, his voice choked with blood in his throat.

Lord Drummond and Andrew had moved away and so did not hear the last words of Lord Ashley.

'I want the child brought up as I have done,' he croaked. 'She must never be revealed as a girl.'

'I understand,' the gentleman replied.

One man with a torch showed Lord Drummond the way to his coach, where Benson took over.

'A sad end of a happy event, Benson,' said Lord Drummond as he climbed into his coach, followed by Andrew.

'Indeed, my lord,' commented Benson, as he shut the door of the carriage and climbed onto the box.

Andrew looked back but all he could see was a group of torches and two men carrying Lord Ashley's body to his coach. What would Eloise and Carl make of it all, he wondered? He had not seen Carl since the night they had been on the stairs listening to the music. Would they blame him for their father's death? He felt sorry for them, for in the short time he had known the Ashleys he had grown fond of Lady Ashley, Eloise and Carl. The only one he didn't like was Lord Ashley, who had tried to kill him. He wanted to ask his father a lot of questions but the man sat morose and brooding in his corner of the carriage.

It was a long journey and they had to make a stopover at the same hotel where Andrew had first caught sight of Lord Ashley. At dinner that night Lord Drummond told his son, 'We've been neglecting your education, Andrew.'

'Oh,' said Andrew. 'How?'

'I think you should go away to some academy.'

'Oh, no.'

'It is for your own good, Andrew.'

'But I've been doing very well at home. You've taught me a lot. You and Benson and the parson.'

'It's not enough.'

Andrew knew better than to contradict his father. Lord Drummond's idea was that he should begin to go out into the world and meet people. Andrew didn't understand why, but he had to submit, though he didn't look forward to living away from Drummond Castle.

The second part of the journey was tedious. Andrew kept thinking of happy times at Ashley Castle, but even they, he had to admit, had been tainted with some nameless fear. Why had Carl said that he'd pushed him into the lake? They had been playing happily until then. And even after that incident there had been the lovely moment on the landing when Carl had smiled and held his hand as they listened to the musicians below.

His reverie came to an end when he heard his father say, 'At last,' as they drove through the gateway to Drummond Castle. The major-domo came down the steps and opened the door of the carriage, let down the steps and made them welcome with a real, warm smile on his white, round, solid face, the face of the perfect servant.

In the Grand Hall, softly lit and flower-scented, the footmen in green and white livery stood in two rows to give their welcome. Lord Drummond had a word with each one of them, the grand seigneur who had made his way to fortune less with the sword than with his brilliant personality. He would speak to the meanest servant, jocularly, who would never react with disrespect. There was that about Lord Drummond which inspired fear as well as affection. He dismissed the servants with a word.

Andrew made his way to his room and that night, after Benson had administered to his needs, he fell into a deep sleep, untroubled by any echoes of Ashley Castle.

The academy that Andrew was sent to was run by monks, and he spent several unhappy years there, the unhappiness relieved only by holidays spent with his father and Benson at Drummond Castle. Each time he left for the academy he asked his father, 'How much longer?' and each time his father replied 'Not much longer.

He had reached the age of seventeen when he had a rare visit from his father at the academy. That evening Lord Drummond seemed very gay and excited, which was not usual for him. Whenever he had visited his son before, he had been quite subdued and serious. Andrew could not understand the change of mood. They talked about nothing in particular, no mention was made of his future except for Andrew's perpetual question: 'How much longer?' Little did

Andrew know just how short a time he would remain at the academy, for just a few hours after the visit, his father would be fighting for his life, a fight he would lose.

Andrew was told by one of the priests who took him aside that his father had died of wounds sustained in a duel with one of the Ashley family. The priest did not know the cause of the quarrel, but Andrew knew that it would take very little to cause an Ashley to seek vengeance for the death of Lord Ashley at his father's hands.

'So the feud continues,' said Andrew when the priest had finished his story.

'Feud?' questioned the priest.

'The Drummonds and the Ashleys are sworn enemies.'

'What a pity,' said the priest.

That night, in the academy dormitory, Andrew wished that he could talk to old and loyal Benson. There was no one at the academy that he could tell how he felt or what he was thinking. He did not weep for his father; his grief was too deep for that.

He wasn't a very good student and after the death of his father he was even worse, but the monks seemed to understand and did not chastise him in any way.

His sojourn at the academy was terminated one day when the Drummond carriage pulled up in the driveway and Andrew was summoned to appear.

'Get in,' was all Benson said.

Andrew obediently climbed into the carriage. Benson climbed up onto the box and urged the two greys into a trot, leaving the priests on the doorsteps of the academy wondering what on earth could happen next in their unreal world.

No words were exchanged between Andrew and Benson until they arrived at Drummond Castle, not a long way from the academy. There was no parade of footmen and servants as there had been whenever Andrew arrived with his father. As he got down from the carriage and stood looking up at the castle, he asked, 'Where is everybody?'

'I told them to keep out of the way,' said Benson. 'I didn't think you'd want to be reminded...'

Andrew did not comment. With a lump in his throat he climbed the steps and entered the castle, followed by Benson. He made for the library which his father had always used as a study.

'Come in, Benson,' he commanded.

Andrew sat in his father's desk chair. He did not invite Benson to sit down.

'Tell me what happened.'

'It was at a shooting party. A cousin of Lord Ashley picked a quarrel and that was that.'

'I suppose that boy Carl is now Lord Ashley,' said Andrew.

'I suppose so, sir. But I understand the Ashleys are in a bad way financially since Lord Ashley was killed.'

'Did my father. . . ?' Andrew hesitated as he choked on the words. 'Did my father . . . say anything?'

'Yes, sir. He did.'

'Was there a message for me?'

'There were what you might call instructions.'

'Oh?'

Benson took a crumpled piece of paper from his tunic pocket.

'Is that his writing?'

'No, sir. It's mine.'

'Go on.'

'Your father wants you to give up living at the castle and stay with your guardian in London.'

'Give up the castle?'

'That's what he said. He doesn't mean forever. He means for the time being.'

'But why?'

'He thought it would have unhappy memories for you.'

'Guardian? I didn't know I had a guardian.'

'Oh, yes. Your father arranged it when he knew he had to fight that man.'

'Who is this guardian?'

Benson consulted his piece of paper. 'Lord Evesham. He's a very nice man. You'll like him. I am to drive you to London to meet him.'

'I don't want to go to London.'

'It is your father's wish, my lord.'

'What? What did you say?' Andrew was puzzled by the title.

'You are now Lord Drummond, sir.'

'Oh. Yes. I suppose I am.'

'Your father gave me strict instructions. I was to look after you as usual and try to help you in your grief.'

'I don't think you'll be able to do that, Benson,' muttered Andrew. 'He was my father and I loved him.'

'So did I,' said Benson. 'Very much.'

Andrew got up from the desk and moved across the room to look out of the window. Still looking out of the window, he said, 'Oh dear, Benson. What am I going to do without him?'

'You're going to be a man to start with, my lord, so that your father can be proud of you.'

'Yes,' Andrew whispered. 'Show me where he's buried.'

They both left the room and went outside the castle to a part of the grounds that had been set aside many years ago for the burial of members of the Drummond line. Benson led Andrew to a newly dug grave next to that of the boy's mother.

'Oh, they're together at last.'

'Yes, my lord.'

As they stood looking down at the grave Andrew asked, 'What else did my father say?'

'He was anxious that you should spend your next few years with your guardian for what he called social reasons. He thought you would not want to use the castle again until you were married.'

'Married?'

'That's what he said.'

'Then we must respect his wishes.'

'Yes, my lord.'

As they walked away Andrew realised that he could not be happy in the castle without his father. He would call on Lord Evesham. He realised that although he was eighteen years of age, he was legally a minor and his finances would be controlled until he reached his majority.

Drummond Castle was not a long way from London. At least it was near enough to avoid an overnight stay on the way, unlike Ashley Castle that was less accessible to the capital. Andrew wondered why, with the two families so far apart, the feud should continue. How the Ashley cousin had managed to meet his father was a mystery unless, of course, it was pre-arranged. Recalling the subterfuge of the so-called Reconciliation Ball which had turned out to be a failed opportunity to dispose of Andrew himself he realised that it was not beyond the bounds of possibility that this unknown cousin had gone out of his way to avenge the death of Lord Ashley. Now that both Lord Drummond and Lord Ashley had been eliminated, the feud might die down, for the only combatants left were himself and Carl, the new Lord Ashley. He wondered where he was, for he still harboured some affection for the boy.

Benson guided the horses into the gravel carriageway of a large house bordering an ornamental park in a luxurious quarter of London where several such mansions were situated.

Andrew found it difficult to reconcile Lord Evesham with any cousinship to his father. This man was a dilettante, almost a fop; dark and distinctly handsome, he walked with an ornamental cane, not because he was in need of it though he was much older than Andrew's father, but for the mere cosmetic effect.

Every room in the house was large with tall ceilings. There was a large garden with a lake and stabling in a mews nearby. Andrew was shown into the library where he was to meet this man whom he could only regard as a bit of fop. A seventy-year-old fop. They shook hands and Andrew noticed afterwards that his own hand had become perfumed by the contact.

'Sit down, my boy,' said Lord Evesham in a voice that belied his appearance. Andrew decided that he was a man not to be thwarted.

'Your father appointed me your guardian, Andrew,' he went on. 'I suppose you know what that means?'

27

'Yes, sir,' said Andrew.

Lord Evesham threw up his well-manicured hands in mock alarm.

'Oh, don't call me that. Call me Eve. Everybody else does.'

'I will, in future, sir. I mean, Eve.'

'How old are you?'

'Eighteen.'

'Ah. Yes. Well, the first thing to do is to show you over the house, which I will do myself. So come.'

He stood up and led Andrew out of the room. They did a complete tour of the house which was truly magnificent. Andrew had expected the old man to be breathless and fatigued, but he wasn't. He obviously loved the house and loved showing it off. Andrew was more than happy with what he saw. His own quarters occupied a complete floor and were self-contained. Benson would be accommodated in the servants quarters. Andrew thought that living with a guardian would entail living in the man's lap, so to speak, but it was obvious that Eve valued his own freedom as much as Andrew did his. He would be able to spend as much of his time with Benson as he wanted. He had his own dining room but could eat with Eve any time he wanted to, and although Andrew and his father had never worried very much about food, Eve's idea of a meal was an event even when he was on his own, which was seldom.

Andrew very soon had experience of Eve's way of living, for he had arranged for the two of them to dine together, and this entailed a vast array of dishes served by immaculate servants. The wine, to which Andrew was not accustomed, was so selected as to cause him neither discomfort nor embarrassment.

Andrew soon realised that he was going to enjoy himself. From now on, according to Eve, he was to burst his sheath and become a dragonfly, whatever the old man meant by that. Andrew was to discover that his guardian was inclined, without warning, to indulge in flamboyant language. He was a well read, cultured gentleman, keen on observing the same impeccable behaviour in others that he practised himself. He told Andrew that he was a very rich young man and that he himself would govern his yearly allowance until he became of age, but would not deprive him of any expenditure that he might need from time to time. He realised, he said, that young men were inclined to need extra money now and then. This was a hint that Andrew might procure a mistress of some kind, an idea that never entered his head. Eve also insisted that Andrew visit his tailor for a completely new wardrobe. Living in London, Eve explained, was very different from living in the country.

'You can forget all you learnt at that academy, my boy,' he exclaimed. 'That's all right for children. It's very easy to be a saint in a monastery but it's difficult to be a gentleman in London.'

Evidence of this was apparent the next day when Eve had arranged for Andrew to be presented to some of his friends at a lunch at the Cafe Royal.

Fourteen people besides Andrew had been invited to the repast. Six of the guests were ladies, very great ladies to Andrew's simple eyes. Had he known more of the world he might have wondered at the disposition of the guests, for a very old gentleman, to whom he had been introduced but whose name he had forgotten, sat between two duchesses; and the rest of the illuminati sat, three of them all together in one group and the sixth on the right hand of his guardian. He wondered who should occupy such an exalted position. One thing struck him especially among the male guests. They all had a languid air not dissimilar to that of his guardian, the half-lisp, the attentive-inattentive manner of the dilettante.

With the fish course the conversation became more general, and with the iced champagne, served from jeroboams that took two men to lift, decency seemed to depart. It was strange to Andrew, as an observer, to see these men forgetting themselves, to see languid faces become flushed, to hear soft voices become harsh, tongues become ribald, all induced by alcohol.

At the head of the table, only a hint more flushed than

29

usual, sat Lord Evesham, also observing the changes that Andrew noticed. They had all sat down at table, apparently staid and respectable, but by degrees had become crowing cocks and baying asses, the high, harsh laughter of the ladies filling the air. Sober himself, self-contained and courtly, Sir Evesham seemed to emanate calmness.

In the midst of the smoke and chatter he rose with a glass of champagne between two fingers as a lady might hold a rose, and proposed Andrew's health and success in society. After he sat down Andrew got to his feet. He had no idea what to say. He thanked his guardian for all that he had done for him. He couldn't help saying that he wished his father had been able to propose the toast, which his guardian applauded. Before he had finished speaking, one of the lady guests fell back in her chair and onto the floor, taking the tablecloth with her as she clutched it to save herself. Andrew sat down with everyone laughing and jumping up to help the stricken lady.

When it was over Andrew and Eve waited to bid farewell to the guests, shaking hands and kissing cheeks. Half an hour later Eve and Andrew were walking arm in arm through the London streets. Eve was pleased, very pleased. He told Andrew that he had conducted himself in a modest and becoming manner. They didn't walk far, the whole purpose of the perambulation being for the benefit of Eve to express his approbation out of earshot. That achieved, they turned round and went back to the Cafe Royal to pick up their carriage. As they were driving home Eve said 'I have to go out tonight. I'm dining with the Duke of Buckingham. You don't mind being left alone, do you?'

'No. No,' replied Andrew. 'Not at all. I'd like to sort myself out.'

He would also need to recover from such a lunch.

'You can please yourself now, you know,' added Eve. 'You've got plenty of money and the whole world is waiting for you. So try to enjoy yourself.'

'I will.'

As Andrew, with the help of Benson, was settling into his

extensive quarters in Walpole House, as the house was called, Andrew couldn't help wondering how the old man, as he thought of his guardian, could suffer another mammoth repast with the Duke of Buckingham. It seemed to be his life: eating, drinking, socialising. What would Andrew's life be in contrast? He had enjoyed the celebratory lunch but he couldn't do it every day. As for twice a day, that would be impossible. So it would appear that Andrew was faced with a life of idleness. How to occupy his days and nights? He had no hobbies except for painting. He had started drawing at the academy and the monks, although they condemned such material manifestations, conceded that he had some talent, particularly when the subject matter appealed to them, as when he painted some ecclesiastical vision or a re-enactment of some story from the bible.

It was only natural, then, that in his many idle moments he should turn to painting. Much to Benson's embarrassment he did a portrait of him which, when it was completed, turned out to be more flattering than embarrassing and Benson kept it hidden, though treasured.

Apart from such occasional excursions into the world of art, it was doubtful if a more forlorn character than Andrew could be found in the whole of London. With as much money as anyone could want and with the whole of London society to call upon, he took to exploring London on foot, weather permitting.

One evening he went out intending to dine somewhere quiet and watch the world go by. It was an evening he would remember because Fate, or whatever it is called, took a hand in his life and changed everything, giving him a reason for living, his life of idleness abandoned.

High above him hung the evening sky. Over in the west, clouds were brilliant and liquid, creating a topaz-coloured sunset. London was preparing for the night, wrapping herself in the dark gauze of shadows and spangling herself with lights.

Andrew found himself on the Embankment where he lingered, gazing at the water of the Thames and listening to the sounds of the city. Then he walked on. He found himself in a busy thoroughfare with a blaze of lights where there were cafes, the music of a barrel organ and a crowd of people. There were men with long hair behaving like dandies, men in peg-top trousers, wearing smoking caps with tassels and smoking long pipes. There were men in rags, hawkers selling their wares, a blind man tapping his way with a white stick, ordinary men and women, some of them with ghostlike faces, some with faces like roses. Squalor and beauty all drifting together as if blown by the wind of the summer night, here in shadow, here in blazing light. It was a fantastic sight to find in London.

It fascinated Andrew and, mixing with the throng, he drifted with them. He came to a halt where a man had placed a square of carpet on the pavement on which, lit by a lantern, two tiny dolls, manipulated by an invisible thread, were dancing and tumbling to the delight of a small crowd of onlookers.

Tiring of the antics of the dolls, Andrew studied the small audience. One of them was a man with a violin tucked under his arm, a man with a round, fresh-looking, childlike face. Andrew thought he knew that face and stood browsing and watching the man who was absorbed in the dancing dolls. Then it came to him. The man had not changed in the years since Andrew had first seen him as he and Carl and Eloise peered through the banisters at Ashley Castle. The man seemed to be aware that Andrew was staring at him and turned to look idly in his direction. There was no recognition on the man's part. How could there be? How could he connect the child in its nightgown with the fashionable young man staring at him now? As he moved away Andrew accosted him.

'Excuse me, sir,' he said.

The violinist stopped in his tracks.

'I believe,' Andrew went on, 'I have had the pleasure of your acquaintance though we have never spoken to each other.'

The man smiled nervously and fidgeted with his violin case as he ransacked his memory.

'I don't recall,' he said.

Andrew laughed as he explained, 'You may not remember me but I certainly remember you.'

'I travel a lot, of course,' said the man.

'It was a long time ago,' said Andrew. 'At Ashley Castle.'

'Ashley Castle?'

'I was watching you through the banisters on the landing and there was another little boy and a girl with me.'

'Yes. Yes,' exclaimed the violinist, suddenly. 'There was a child in the gallery. That was you?'

'Yes.

The man looked Andrew up and down. He was too astounded to say anything for a moment. The obvious difference in their circumstances, emphasised by their clothing, confused the simple mind of the violinist. Then he passed a hand over his face as if wiping away the intervening years.

'How amazing,' he murmured.

'How amazing indeed!' laughed Andrew. 'You see I do not forget my friends.'

'Friends?' queried the man. As if in embarrassment he, too, laughed.

Andrew managed to persuade the violinist to join him in a dinner at one of the brightly lit cafes. He did not want to lose sight of him. He was a slender but important connection with the past which meant so much to him, the past that included his father, Carl and Eloise, all long lost.

While they were waiting for their food, Andrew could not help but notice how threadbare his friend's clothes were. His coat was old and frayed yet he still managed to appear well-dressed. He was also very hungry and obviously enjoyed his food. After a glass of wine both men became convivial. Andrew told his friend, whose name was Franz, about the feud between the Drummonds and the Ashleys, how Lord Ashley had tried to murder him, how his father had fought him in a duel and killed him only to be killed himself later by another member of the Ashley family.

'Good Heavens,' exclaimed Franz.

What else could he say? He was listening to a young man

who was pouring out his thoughts as though he were desperate to talk to somebody. Andrew talked as though he were glad to remember the past, including the tragedies. He then told Franz about the myth of Carl being a girl who had been brought up as a boy because of Lord Ashley's obsession with the ancient murder. Andrew admitted that he didn't believe in the myth and Franz agreed with him. In fact they both laughed at the thought.

Encouraged by the conviviality of the occasion, Franz told Andrew his own story. He had evidently belonged to a band of wandering minstrels and had come upon Ashley Castle by accident. They had got lost and called at the castle on an off chance. They had been lucky and were even kept after the ball to play in the drawing room. That was when Andrew had seen them. Once the minstrels had left the castle they made their way to London where they went their separate ways. Franz was now part of an orchestra that played for dances. In fact, he had been on his way to an engagement when Andrew accosted him.

Andrew enjoyed the encounter so much that he hated the idea of parting from Franz. He was a reminder of things outside London and Andrew never considered himself a city man in any way.

'We mustn't lose touch, Franz,' he said, earnestly.

'It's very kind of you, sir,' replied Franz. 'But I'm afraid I'm a bit of a night bird in my business.'

'Do you mean you sleep all day?'

'Most mornings. I'm playing until the early hours, you see.'

'Where are you off to now?'

'We're playing at the Empress Hall.'

'What's on there?'

'Arts students' Fancy Dress Ball. A very lively affair, as a rule.'

'Really?'

'They had to call in the militia last year.'

'Oh, dear. If it wasn't Fancy Dress I'd come with you.'

'You are in Fancy Dress,' said Franz.

'What do you mean?'

'No offence meant, but compared to the people there, you would not be out of place dressed as an aristocrat.'

Andrew looked down at himself.

'You could be right. We have a lot to talk about, Franz. We could meet during the interval.'

'Of course.'

'Come on, then,' urged Andrew. 'Let's go.'

They got up from the table and made their way to the Empress Hall. When they got there, people were arriving in droves, wearing all sorts of costumes. And there was a great deal of noise as the students, male and female, called to each other excitedly. Andrew saw a Japanese carrying a lantern and, of course, there was a Satan and quite a few fairies complete with wings, a shepherdess, a soldier.

Andrew went inside with the collection of students, not looking at all out of place in his costume, while Franz went in by another entrance to join up with his fellow musicians.

Inside the vast hall everything was bright and noisy. There was colour and laughter, for some of the students had erected tableaux and amusing decorations. Andrew heard the band tuning up and leaned against a wall to survey the scene around him.

What a sight! Everybody was young. All were students, of course. There were monkey costumes, Pierrots and Pierrettes and girls dressed as dominoes. The band broke into a waltz and set the whole fantastic crowd whirling. A girl dressed as a bon-bon danced up to Andrew, did a high kick and danced off again with someone representing a large carrot. Andrew suddenly felt lost and out of place.

He was still standing there against the wall when a fresh explosion of guests burst into the hall, two men and three girls, all evidently friends, linked together arm in arm. It was as well that Andrew was leaning against the wall, because one of the girls could have been taken for Eloise Ashley, changed from the frilly pantalooned child into a girl of eighteen, laughing and joyous. Andrew gazed in wonder at this prodigy who was now whirling before him in the waltz in the arms of a handsome grenadier, totally unconscious of the turmoil her appearance had stirred in him.

The bon-bon girl came up to Andrew and disturbed his vacant musings.

'Aren't you dancing?' she asked.

'Not at the moment,' Andrew replied.

'Come!' she commanded and pulled him onto the dance floor.

The girl did not seem to be in demand as a partner herself, the reason, Andrew soon discovered, being her habit of returning to the bar after each dance, though she was far from intoxicated. Andrew was polite to her but scarcely needed her as his mind was absorbed by the marvellous girl who looked so much like Eloise. He asked his bon-bon partner if she knew her.

'Know her?' the girl cried, a little too loudly for Andrew's liking. 'Everybody knows her. Her name's Marie. She's a model. All the students know her and all the artists in the neighbourhood have used her. You don't want anything to do with her.'

'Why not?' Andrew asked.

'She's common,' said the girl, dismissively, in a voice that could not have sounded more common.

The ball inevitably became infected by the element of riot. Students traditionally and by inclination were unable to conduct themselves in a sober fashion. Scarcely had the music ceased than there came shrill screams, shouts and sounds of scuffling. The grenadier and the giant carrot were engaged in what would appear to be mortal combat, obviously caused by some disagreement over a girl. A ring of shouting spectators surrounded the two men, and in the midst of the throng stood the shepherdess, weeping. This was the girl called Marie, the girl so like Eloise of Ashley Castle. To add to the confusion caused by the fisticuffs in the middle of the floor, some of the students had grabbed the instruments from the members of the orchestra and were blowing trumpets in raucous abandon. There was a crash of broken glass, and chairs and benches were turned over as the riot grew.

Andrew rushed forward and grabbed the shepherdess by

the hand, pulling her away and out of the hall into the street. She did not resist. She was no longer crying, she was too frightened. They moved down the street and she and Andrew took refuge in the first cafe they came to. As the girl sat down, exhausted, she asked, 'Is my dress torn?'

'No. It's all right,' Andrew assured her. He ordered hot chocolate and cakes which the girl pounced upon.

'Who are you?' she asked, eventually. 'And what does your costume represent?'

'I represent an aristocrat,' said Andrew quickly, not wishing to disclose his name.

'I saw you looking at me in there. Your eyes seemed to follow me the whole evening.'

'You attracted me.'

'You know,' she announced thoughtfully, 'I think I've seen you before.'

'Do you?'

'Or you remind me of someone.'

'Do I?'

Then they were silent.

'You are not eating, Mr Aristocrat,' she said. 'What's the matter with you?'

'I'm not hungry.'

'We're always hungry,' she said and laughed.

'Are you sure your name is Marie?' he asked.

'Yes,' she replied. 'It's my professional name. I'm a model. We all have professional names. It makes us easier to find.'

Andrew decided not to pursue the subject as it obviously embarrassed her. The very embarrassment itself only increased his curiosity.

When the girl had finished eating, Andrew decided to see her home for her own protection. As they were walking towards her lodgings she asked, 'Do you like my costume?'

'It's very nice,' said Andrew.

'Oh, how dull you are, Mr Artistocrat,' cried the girl. 'You should have said "my dear, your costume is charming". Go on, say it.'

'My dear, your costume is charming,' repeated Andrew, dutifully.

'Is that the best you can do?' complained the girl. 'You sound like an undertaker.'

Andrew knew at that moment, without any doubt, that the girl who called herself Marie was in fact Eloise, daughter of Lord and Lady Ashley and Carl's sister. She had used exactly the same words about her dress and in the same coquettish way as when they had first met at Ashley Castle. How could he forget? She might call herself Marie but she was Eloise as well.

They turned down a narrow side street. The girl stopped at a dark door and took a key from her pocket.

'Is this it?' asked Andrew, looking up at the dreary building.

'Yes,' she said resignedly. 'This is it!'

'Don't go,' pleaded Andrew. 'I must see you again.'

'Oh, they all say that,' muttered the girl.

The door was open now and she made to enter the building. Andrew reached out and grabbed her wrist.

'No,' he exclaimed.

The girl was suddenly afraid and pulled her arm away.

'You're hurting,' she cried.

'Eloise,' said Andrew.

The girl went limp. She ceased to struggle and looked at Andrew in a startled way.

'What did you say?' she asked weakly.

'Have you forgotten Handy Andy?' Andrew asked her.

'Andrew!' she shrieked. 'Where . . . ?'

She couldn't go on as recollections rushed upon her, tears welling in her eyes.

'Ashley Castle,' he reminded her. 'The pine forest and little Carl who fell in the lake.'

'You!' she cried in disbelief.

'I never thought I'd see you again,' said Andrew. 'And now that I've found you I can't let you go.'

They stood gazing at each other.

'Come upstairs,' said Eloise, turning and climbing the uncarpeted stairs. She led the way to a bare, poorly furnished room lit by the bright moonlight outside. She turned and clung to Andrew, sobbing.

'Oh, Andrew. It's been so horrible,' she sobbed.

Andrew led her to sit down on the side of the little iron bedstead. He sat beside her, holding her hand while the sobs racked her body.

'I knew you,' she said. 'I knew you from somewhere. I didn't know where. How could I?'

Through the miserable veils that lay between her and that happy time the past seemed as vague to her as a dream. Gradually the sad tale unfolded itself. When Lord Ashley died at the hands of Andrew's father, it was discovered that he was so heavily in debt that everything had to be given up, including the castle. She and her mother had lived as best they could, begging their way to London where they lived in slums. It was the old, old story that made you wonder if there was a God. The beautiful Lady Ashley had suffered terribly and died one very cold winter. At someone's suggestion Eloise, left alone, became an artists' model because of her beauty and her figure, all of which led to the wretched room in which they were now sitting, clinging to each other as if they were children again. It seemed that, in spite of her hardships, Eloise was still in heart and spirit as she had been then. She had never grown up. Life had overtaken her.

'And little Carl?' asked Andrew. 'What happened to him?'

'He was taken away by Father's cousin. I don't know what happened to him or where he is. Abroad, I expect.'

'That was probably the cousin who killed my father in a duel.'

'Oh, no!' cried Eloise. 'Not another one.'

'I'm afraid so. The feud still goes on.'

'Not with us. Not with us, Andrew.'

'No. Not with us.'

'Poor Carl. He was such a troubled creature.'

'I grew very fond of him,' said Andrew simply.

'He was very pretty,' admitted Eloise.

'I suppose the Ashleys still think I'm going to kill him.'

'What about you, Andrew? What's happened to you?'

'When my father died I came to London to live with my guardian, Lord Evesham.'

'You're rich?'

'Well, yes. I suppose so.'

'We lost all our money. Poor Mother. How she suffered!'

'Didn't Carl want to stay with you, so you could all be together?'

'Mother couldn't afford it.'

'He's Lord Ashley now, of course.'

'Yes. And you're Lord Drummond.'

'Yes.'

'What were you doing at the ball?'

'Do you remember Franz?'

'Who?'

'No. You wouldn't know his name. You remember we watched the musicians through the banisters at Ashley Castle?'

'With Carl. Yes.'

'Franz was the violinist and I met him in the street this evening. He told me he was playing at the ball, so I went along with him just for something to do.'

'And you found me.'

'Yes. And that reminds me. I lost sight of Franz and I don't know his address.'

'Don't worry. Someone at the ball will know it.'

'Eloise,' said Andrew suddenly. 'What are we going to do? You can't stay here. You must leave it.'

'I can't. I can't afford to. Everybody knows I'm here whenever there's work.'

'I won't let you stay here.'

'Where can I go?'

'To the country.'

'The country? I doubt if I'll ever see that again.' Eloise's despair was almost tangible.

'I will arrange it,' Andrew assured her.

'How? What can you do?'

'I'll buy a house in the country and you can live in it as long as you like.'

'Oh, Andrew. If only that were possible.'

'Eloise, I will make it possible. You can come and live in my guardian's house until I find the house for you.'

'Oh, could I?'

'Of course.'

'What about your guardian?'

'I have my own quarters and there are plenty of rooms.'

'Oh, Andrew!'

She began to cry again.

'What are you crying for now?' asked Andrew, puzzled.

'Because I'm happy,' she cried. 'For the first time for so long.'

Andrew could not explain his own feelings, he couldn't put them into words if he tried. A little while ago he had been wondering what he was going to do with himself, with his time, his life. A little painting, he thought. But now he'd found someone he could help. He intended to look after Eloise as much as she would let him.

It was late when he left her miserable lodgings and he promised to collect her the next day. He found the streets almost empty as he made his way back to his own house.

What was he going to do with Eloise? That was the question he kept asking himself. He was not in love with her. Of that he was certain. If he was in love with anyone it was Carl, but in no way homosexually. He still thought of him as a very attractive boy. Carl obviously called himself Lord Ashley. Andrew did not think of Eloise in the same way as he thought of Carl. He was fond of her and wanted to protect her, even though she was an Ashley and his historical enemy. He was hardly conscious of that factor or perhaps he simply ignored it. He didn't know which. To him Eloise was the little girl who had escorted him through the portrait gallery at Ashley Castle.

Benson was waiting up for him when he arrived home. 'I thought you'd got lost,' he remarked.

'No, Benson. As a matter of fact, I found myself.' That was just how he felt. He had found a purpose in life and did not feel as useless as when he had set out earlier that evening.

41

'It's too late for riddles,' grumbled Benson. He wanted to go to bed but Andrew detained him.

'Do you remember the little Ashley girl when we were there, Benson?' he asked.

'Vaguely.'

'I met her tonight.'

'Who?'

'Eloise.'

'So that's where you were.'

'You remember the musicians that night at Ashley Castle?'

'Yes. I remember them.'

'I met one of them in the street tonight.'

'You have been busy, my lord.'

'It was quite by accident. His name is Franz and he was playing at a students' ball so I went along with him. That's where I met Eloise.'

'She's a student, is she?'

'No. She's a model. You know. Artist's model.'

'Oh,' said Benson, ominously.

'Why do you say it like that?' Andrew asked, suspiciously.

'You know what they say about artist's models, sir.'

'No. I don't. You must tell me in the morning, Benson. I'm tired. Goodnight.'

'Goodnight, my lord.'

Benson worried as he made his way wearily to bed. He hoped that his master was not going to get himself involved in any unpleasantness. The feud between the two families was bad enough, but to get tied up with an artist's model could only make matters worse. The Ashley girl might be everything that was sweet and lovely but models, as those in servants' quarters well knew, had a reputation. Benson knew, from reliable gossip, that the Ashleys had suffered terrible financial disasters and that the family had broken up. Lady Ashley had died in complete poverty and the girl, he now learned, had become a model, but no one seemed to know what had become of the boy, Lord Ashley. It was a tragedy but Benson could not feel sorry for any of them. After all, they had killed his old master and had tried to murder his new one.

That night Andrew dreamt of little Carl. He still called him little Carl, though Andrew knew that he must be of a similar age as himself if he was still alive. In the dream Carl was wearing a splendid uniform and represented some foreign country. On waking, Andrew could only hope that the boy was still alive. He could not interpret the dream. He could not tell if it meant that Carl was alive or dead. The boy could have gone abroad, of course, as Eloise suggested. Andrew had found Eloise, but the chance of finding Carl was very remote.

Andrew did not meet his guardian at breakfast. Lord Evesham never came downstairs to breakfast but had something in his room. He did not appear downstairs until eleven o'clock at the earliest, when he drank a glass of champagne. Andrew found him in the drawing room seated in a large wing armchair, glass in hand.

'Good morning, Andrew,' he drawled.

'Good morning, Eve. Did you have a pleasant evening with the Duke?'

'Very. And very late.'

'I was rather late myself,' Andrew admitted.

'Oh?' Eve was not particularly curious.

'I thought I'd try and discover London,' Andrew explained.

'It's already been discovered, dear boy.'

'I just walked.'

'Not into trouble, I trust.'

'No. But I met a couple of old friends.'

'Good.'

'Friends I hadn't seen for years.'

'Good.'

Eve was beginning to find his young ward's recitation tedious.

'You remember the Ashleys?'

'Of course I do.'

'I met the daughter last night.'

'I thought they'd vanished from the face of the earth,' declared Eve.

'The mother died in poverty.'

43

'Yes. Old Lord Ashley would have gone to prison if your father hadn't killed him.'

'Poor Lady Ashley,' mused Andrew. 'She was very beautiful.'

'She was that.'

'She didn't want the feud to continue.'

'She couldn't stop it. Otherwise your father...' Eve checked himself.

'Oh, I know,' conceded Andrew. 'There will always be someone trying to pick a quarrel. As I'm the only Drummond left, I suppose I should keep my sword arm in trim.'

'I don't suppose this daughter you met would bother to challenge you.'

'Hardly. Since her mother died she's been living as best she can.'

'Don't tell me she's gone on the . . .'

Before his guardian could suggest some sordid career that Eloise might have adopted, Andrew cut him short.

'She's been eking out a living as an artist's model.'

'Poor child,' was Eve's only reluctant comment.

'I hadn't seen her since I was at Ashley Castle, mused Andrew. He wanted to tell his guardian of his plan for Eloise but he hesitated. After a brief silence Eve anticipated his ward's intention.

'So you've arranged to see the girl again, have you?' he asked.

'Yes.'

Andrew drew a chair close to Eve, sat down and leaned forward eagerly.

'I want to buy a place in the country and put her in it,' he declared.

'Make her your mistress, you mean?'

'No! I'm not in love with her.'

'You don't have to be.'

'It's not that.'

'You want to tuck her away somewhere. I can understand that.'

44

'I don't want to tuck her away. I want her to have a bit of peace.'

'And give up modelling.'

'Yes.'

'Is she going to be in this country cottage, or whatever it is, on her own?'

'Well, yes.'

'You'll visit her, of course.'

'Sometimes.

'Are you sure you're not committing her to solitary confinement? It would be rather a strain after her life with students and artists, wouldn't it?'

Andrew seemed to lose some of his enthusiasm.

'She's not happy where she is. She doesn't like modelling and she doesn't like the students. Of course, any time she wants to return to London, I'll find her a place.'

'You don't think you should do that now?'

'I'll leave it to her. I did tell her she could stay here until I found a house.'

'Oh, you did.'

'I have room in my quarters.'

'I know you have.'

'Do you mind?'

'You could have asked me before you told her,' Eve admonished. 'But of course I don't mind so long as she's clean and quiet.'

'I can guarantee that.'

'You realise that you are consorting with the enemy,' Eve reminded him.

'Enemy?'

'She's still an Ashley.'

'Oh, she's not like that. Neither was her mother. That was all Lord Ashley's doing.'

'Sufficient to kill your father, Andrew.'

'Then we're equal. We've each had a father killed in a duel.'

'And the boy? Carl? He's still at large somewhere.'

'Well, yes. But nobody knows where. He's probably abroad.'

45

'It's obvious that it is the male element of the Ashley clan that seeks revenge or whatever they like to call it, and all the time this Carl is alive, the threat still exists.'

'But it doesn't alter the fact that I want to help Eloise.'

'No. I take it you'll be giving the girl some kind of allowance.'

'I hadn't got that far, but you must tell me what you think I can afford.'

'All you need consider is a clothes allowance until you get her into a house where you will have to consider food and staff.'

'Yes. I suppose so.'

'Fortunately you're rich enough to indulge yourself in such whimsical beneficence.'

'There's nothing wrong in wanting to help people, Eve.'

'No. Just don't make it too many or you'll be starting an institution. When do you propose to move this girl in?'

'Today.'

'Don't let me keep you.'

Andrew was dismissed by his guardian, though not unkindly. As he left the room he realised that Eve probably thought him stupid and perhaps he was. He knew little of the world, having only recently left the academy. He was unaware that his actions could be misinterpreted.

He went to find Benson.

'Benson,' he said. 'Bring the carriage round, we're going out.'

'Going out, my lord?' echoed Benson, with relief. 'Where are we going?'

'We're going to rescue Eloise Ashley.'

Benson's attitude changed suddenly. 'My lord, I will bring the carriage round but I will not drive it.'

Andrew was more shocked than annoyed to be so rebuffed. 'Benson! Why not?'

'I'm sorry, my lord. We have known each other a long time, otherwise I would not make so bold as to speak out. I cannot help feeling that no good will come of this Miss Eloise business.'

46

'Go on,' urged Andrew. 'I can see you haven't finished yet.'

'Thank you, my lord. I assure you I mean no offence.'

'I know that, Benson.'

'The Ashleys have not finished with the Drummonds yet, sir.'

'Miss Eloise is not like the other Ashleys.'

'On the night before your father fought with Lord Ashley's cousin, he said that even if he were to fall the next day, the Ashleys would not have done with us. He said Fate had been working against us for over a hundred years. "If I fall", he said, "I rely on you, Benson, to keep my boy away from anyone who has any connection with the Ashleys." '

'He said that?'

'He said that,' repeated Benson. 'And what happens? Your first night of liberty and you meet the Ashley girl. Of all the girls in London, you choose your enemy.'

'She is not my enemy but if you refuse to help me, Benson, then you are.'

'I'm sorry to hear that, sir.'

'I'm sorry to have to say it, Benson.'

'What about your father?'

'I think he would understand what I am trying to do.'

'What are you trying to do?'

'Relieve someone of their misery regardless of the enmity of others.'

'In that case, my lord, I remain your faithful servant.'

'Thank you, Benson.' Then he added, 'My friend.'

As Benson left to attend to the carriage, Andrew sent a servant to the Empress Hall to find out the address of Franz, the violinist. He was determined to keep in touch with those with connections to Ashley Castle, in spite of his father's fears. Franz was another one who could obviously do with some help.

To Andrew's great surprise, his guardian came to visit him in his quarters. Eve immediately made himself at home, spreading himself in one of the armchairs.

'This is an honour, Eve,' said Andrew in welcome.

'Don't be so pedantic, boy.'

47

'Welcome, anyway.'

'I have news for you, Andrew.'

'Yes?'

'There is a house for sale on the Thames near Windsor. I suggest you go and see it as soon as possible.'

'Thank you. I will. Have you the address?'

'Here.

He handed Andrew a piece of paper with the address written on it. With that, he got out of the chair and prepared to leave.

'That's all,' he said, abruptly.

'Thank you again.'

'Your carriage appears to be at the door,' said Eve, as he was leaving.

Andrew went down to find that his carriage was indeed waiting. He gave Benson Eloise's address as a footman from the house helped him inside. With Benson on his box in charge of the two greys, they set off.

It would be difficult for the worldly minded to understand Andrew's happiness as he made his way to rescue Eloise. Not that he considered himself anything of a philanthropist. It was just that he had found some purpose in his idle life. He had found someone to cherish. He was not in the least in love with Eloise, but ever since earliest childhood, he had been very much alone in the world. Without knowing it, Andrew had always missed the love of a mother or a sister. Eloise had been the only girl of his own age with whom he had had contact, and although their acquaintance had been short enough, that fact had made her influence upon him doubly potent. And now he had found her again. She was now a woman, but for him she was still the little girl of Ashley Castle and his love for her was that of a brother for a sister.

The carriage turned down the dingy street and both carriage and horses looked completely out of place. As they approached the house Andrew could see Eloise standing on the doorstep. Through the window of the carriage he called out, 'Eloise!'

He was out of the carriage before it had stopped.

'Andy!' cried Eloise, in a voice full of gladness.

As Andrew stood with Eloise on the doorstep, he heard one of the upper windows open and a nasty laugh issue from within. He looked up and recognised one of the students from the night before. He had a cap with a tassel on his head, a long pipe in his mouth and his shirt was none too clean. The student looked down and laughed again, showing his large, yellow teeth.

'Ignore him,' muttered Eloise as Andrew led her to the carriage. She stopped suddenly.

'Wait,' she cried. 'I have to collect my clothes and things.'

'I'll help you,' said Andrew.

Together they entered the smelly building and gathered up what they could of Eloise's belongings, which were piti-fully few. They made their way down from the girl's floor to the street, and as they did so, a door opened on the landing and the pipe smoking student appeared.

'Are you leaving us, Eloise?' he sneered.

Before Eloise could reply, Andrew said, 'Yes. And never coming back.'

'We'll miss you,' he said, chuckling, as the two of them went down the stairs.

Benson helped them into the carriage, closed the door and climbed up onto the box. As they drove away, Andrew said, 'We'll go shopping tomorrow and buy you some new clothes.'

'Oh, Andy,' declared Eloise. 'I can't believe this is happen-ing. I can't believe it's really you. I'm sure I'll wake up in a minute.'

They didn't drive directly to the London house, but took the road to Windsor where Andrew wanted to look at the house that his guardian had told him about. He found it easily enough. It was called Riverside Towers and was quite large, with grounds sloping down to the river where there was a broken-down jetty which had been used for a boat of some kind. Andrew decided that the repair of the jetty would be the first item on his agenda, as it was dangerous at the moment. Unfortunately it was something he kept putting off.

Eloise fell in love with the house. The dining room had a painted ceiling depicting a flock of doves circling in a blue sky. The kitchen was tiled and as clean as a dairy. The bedrooms, white and spotless, were simply furnished, the hangings in flowered chintz.

It was time to return to London, so back into the carriage they climbed. Eloise was to stay in the London house until the business of renting the riverside home had been concluded. Eloise's cup of happiness was full.

Arrived back in London, Andrew introduced Eloise to his guardian.

'This is the girl I told you about, Eve,' explained Andrew.

'And very pretty, too,' enthused Eve.

'Thank you, sir,' said Eloise.

'Have you seen the house? Riverside Towers?' Eve asked.

'I took Eloise to see it on the way here,' explained Andrew. 'We both like it and I'll arrange to rent it.'

'Good. You think you'll be happy there, Eloise?'

'I'm sure of it.'

'Well, make yourself at home while you're here.'

'Thank you, sir.'

'You and I must have a little talk later, Andrew,' said Eve.

'Yes. Of course. I'll come and see you once I've settled Eloise in.'

Lord Evesham waved his hand in dismissal, rising out of his chair out of courtesy to the lady.

Once settled in her rooms, Eloise could not thank Andrew enough. She gave him a moist kiss such as children give, flinging her arms round him and squeezing him. Andrew extricated himself and escaped to his guardian's quarters.

'I have an idea you're worried about what I'm doing,' he told Eve.

'Not so much worried as curious. Tell me. Why are you doing all this?'

'All what? I've met a couple of old friends, that's all.'

'Old friends? For how long did you know Eloise?'

'A few days at Ashley Castle years ago.'

'That's all?'

'They were happy days until Lord Ashley tried to suffocate me. I'd never been so happy as I was at the castle with Eloise and Carl. You see, I had company. They were my company. I'd been on my own for so many years. I had someone to play with.'

'And you still want to play with them. Is that it? Or do you want to go round the world doing good deeds?'

'Is that wrong?'

'I don't see any wings sprouting on your shoulders.'

'Perhaps I'm merely indulging in nostalgia.'

'Not indulging. You're wallowing, dear boy.'

'What's the use of having money if you can't use it?'

'Most men like to keep it for their wives.'

'I haven't got a wife.'

'Not at the moment.'

'When that time comes, I will have to think again.'

'And the people you are helping at the moment will find themselves cast off.'

'No. I won't let that happen.'

'Your wife may have something to say about that.'

'Then she wouldn't be my wife.'

'I can only advise you, Andrew.'

'It's very kind of you.'

'But obviously useless.'

Andrew and his guardian parted amicably, Andrew quite aware that he was causing the older man a good deal of concern. Lord Evesham's concern was more for his ward's position in society than for his indulgence in nostalgia. The impeccable Lord Evesham was aware of the strict code relating to membership of London society and, of course, any slight infringement on Andrew's behalf could reflect equally upon himself. To that extent it could appear that Lord Evesham's concern for his ward was somewhat selfish.

That evening Andrew asked Benson if he knew of anybody who would be prepared to live at Riverside Towers and look after Eloise. Surprisingly, Benson thought he might be able to help. He knew of a couple, middle-aged, who had just lost their jobs due to the death of their employer. They were looking for another position. He would speak to them and see if they would be prepared to leave London.

'After all,' he said, 'the dear child must be looked after.'

Benson wasn't being sarcastic. He, too, had succumbed to the genuine charm of Eloise.

Andrew went to bed happy that night but dreamt that he was fighting a duel with Carl, the result of which was undecided, as he awoke with a start before the end. The dream hadn't frightened him. It had saddened him, because he could not imagine hurting dear Carl. It was a bitter-sweet sadness with which he remembered the dream, and which he remembered Carl.

That morning he had another interview with his guardian. Lord Evesham sent a servant to Andrew's quarters requesting his presence as soon as possible. The guardian had heard rumours at his Club the night before that had disturbed him. The gossip already going around certain circles in London was that the new Lord Drummond had been slumming and had picked up with a girl of doubtful reputation. It would appear that the profession of artist's model was a euphemism for prostitution, or for something very near it.

When Lord Evesham recited the rumour to Andrew, the boy protested, most vigorously. The interview took place in Lord Evesham's bedroom, with Lord Evesham in a large wing chair, his favourite item of furniture, and wearing a quilted dressing gown. His breakfast was on a tray in front of him. He took Andrew's outburst calmly.

'First of all, Andrew,' he said, 'you have taken under your wing, for want of a better expression, the daughter of a fraudster.'

'Eloise can't be held responsible for what her father did any more than Lady Ashley could.'

'You saw what it did to her.'

'Yes. It killed her.'

'And the daughter, in desperation, turned to modelling.'

'You make it sound like prostitution.'

'There are those who see the similarity. For myself, I've

never known any models or artists so I am not in a position to judge.'

'The person you are talking about is under your roof at the moment,' Andrew reminded his guardian.

'I am aware of that,' said Lord Evesham. 'And so are all the gossips in London.'

'Gossips!' exclaimed Andrew contemptuously.

'Yes, young man. You may scoff. But it was gossip that contributed in no small way to the death of Eloise's mother.'

'How do you mean?' asked Andrew.

'Some people are loath to associate, no matter the goodness of heart, with people who are no longer accepted in society.'

'Are you saying that Eloise will not be accepted?'

'In some circles, yes. And that, in due course, will apply to you.'

'I can't believe it.'

'It's not what you believe, Andrew. It's what happens.'

'So Eloise will be ostracised?'

'In some circles, yes. That's why you are so wise in burying her by the river.'

'That was certainly not my reason.'

'Fortuitous, nonetheless.'

'The house by the river was your idea, Eve.'

'I know. I was not unaware that any stigma that attaches to you might also attach to me.'

Andrew laughed. 'Eve, you old cynic,' he accused. 'My only regret is that I wasn't able to offer Lady Ashley my protection.'

'Protection? Is that what you call it? You don't intend to marry this Eloise?'

'Good Heavens, no!'

'Mistress?'

'Certainly not!'

Andrew could see that his guardian was puzzled. Beneath the cynical sophistication was concern for his own social future. Andrew didn't want his guardian excluded from his own select group of friends in society among whom he could count high priests of government and royalty and the diplomatic corps.

'All I'm doing,' explained Andrew, 'is giving the girl a chance to live a life of her own.'

'And any money she may require.'

'Naturally.'

'All very noble for a young man not yet twenty-one, adopting a beautiful young girl of a similar age and giving her a house to live in and expenses.'

'Yes. But I don't feel noble. I just want to do it.'

'Do you know what I don't want to happen, Andrew?'

'No.'

'I don't want you to be laughed at.'

Andrew was too shocked to reply. Laughed at? Because of what he was doing for other people? Did that mean that Eve would be laughed at, too? That's what old Lord Evesham was frightened of, becoming the laughing stock of London society. That, Andrew admitted to himself, would worry him more than people laughing at himself. Lord Evesham was a well known and well loved society figure. Evidently there were certain unwritten rules in society that Andrew knew he was yet to learn. Some of them would be against his nature but he supposed he had to accept them or his rebellion would reflect on his guardian. It hurt him already that Lady Ashley and Eloise should be regarded as outcasts through no fault of their own.

Andrew and Lord Evesham looked at each other, not challengingly but in perplexity.

'I wonder what your father would say,' concluded Eve.

'If Father were alive,' said Andrew, 'I would still be living at Drummond Castle unaware of the terrible plight of Lady Ashley and Eloise and powerless to help.'

With that he left the room and returned to his own quarters to ponder his future. He was aware that his guardian's intention was to introduce him into society and to accompany him to the opera, salon events, balls, receptions and so on. He recalled his academy-leaving lunch and the behaviour of the society guests on that occasion. At the moment it was obvious that his guardian regarded him as a bit of a curiosity, a rebel even.

There was no doubt that Lord Evesham was relieved once Eloise was installed in the riverside residence. His demeanour was lighter. He even joked with Andrew and made silly, facetious remarks, not at all like his normal cynical self.

After a period of idleness Andrew decided to get out of London. He took a picnic to Riverside Towers to surprise Eloise and so that Benson could renew his acquaintance with Mr and Mrs Hawley, who were now looking after the place and Eloise.

It was after ten o'clock when the carriage drove up to the house. Andrew found Eloise on the terrace. She was on her knees, with her back to him doing something with some plants.

'Good morning,' he called.

Eloise scrambled to her feet.

'Andy!' she cried, running to him and flinging her arms round him. 'See!' she said, pointing to one of the beds that decorated the terrace. 'I've been weeding.' She had thrown the weeds onto the paving and no doubt the regular gardener would pick them up.

'Mrs Hawley says I will make a good gardener one day,' she said.

She took Andrew's arm and led him into the house. A perfume of violets filled the drawing room. The place had changed since Andrew last saw it. The subtle hand of a woman had rearranged the furniture, looped back the curtains and arranged them in graceful folds. On one of the sofas was a heap of white material which Eloise swept aside.

'That will be a dress one day,' she explained. 'You'll laugh when you see it. It will be so beautiful.'

'I won't laugh,' Andrew said.

Andrew felt at ease in the house. He rejoiced in the way that Eloise had taken to the new life, and her every gesture and intonation indicated her genuine gratitude. It was a natural exchange between two dear friends. Their relationship could not have been less restrained. She had nothing, but what Andrew had he shared with her. That fact alone made him happy.

'I've brought a picnic,' Andrew said.

'A picnic?' Eloise echoed. 'I love picnics.'

'As it's such a lovely day.'

'Yes. Where shall we go?'

'Let's explore those woods,' suggested Andrew, pointing to a small forest that bordered the grounds of the house.

'Hawley says there's a lake in there,' said Eloise. 'Let's try and find it.'

'All right.'

Andrew fetched the picnic basket and they set off for the woods. As soon as they stepped among the trees they were conscious of the silence. The place was full of leaping lights and liquid shadows. Where the trees were not so dense the sunlight came through the waving branches in dazzling, quivering shafts. Twilit alleys led the eye to open spaces, golden gorse and the misty white of the hawthorn. The place was a treasure trove of beauty and the two of them even had to trample on violets and wild cyclamen to make their way. Andrew forgot his guardian, the covenances and the fact that he had come to man's estate.

Suddenly, as if tired, Eloise sat down on a carpet of violets and put her hands back to support herself.

'Listen,' she said, casting her eyes up to the trembling leaves above. A squirrel, clinging to the bark of a tree nearby watched them with his wary eyes. A large bird, a wood pigeon, broke the silence with a sudden flurry of wings, flying off in fright.

'Listen,' said Eloise again. 'There's a woodpecker. Can you hear him? And a jay,' she added, eagerly. The whole wood sang to the breeze that had suddenly freshened, and the light flashed through the dancing leaves.

They went on and found the lake. Moorhens scuttled away as soon as they appeared and came back leisurely when they sat down and opened the picnic hamper. Eloise couldn't resist throwing bread to the moorhens and watching them scramble for it. Her laughter echoed across the lake.

They had finished eating and were drinking the milk that had been put into empty wine bottles when they heard voices behind them. It was female laughter of a not very musical kind. Andrew couldn't believe his ears. As he sat there, he turned to see Hawley leading the way for two men in livery, carrying between them a large picnic basket. They were heading straight for Andrew and Eloise. Following the basket came a party of ladies and gentlemen, one of whom Andrew recognised as his guardian, Lord Evesham.

The old man, as if touched by the May sunshine, had discarded his usual smart attire and was dressed in a suit of light-coloured material, quite elegant and harmonising with the exquisite outfits of his companions. He wore a flower in his buttonhole and he was walking beside a lady Andrew didn't recognise. He was soon to discover that she was the famous model known as Mystique. The two men who made up the party were lords of the realm. These people had broken through the trees and invaded the innocent paradise that Eloise and Andrew had created.

Suddenly Andrew discerned the motive behind the whole event. This was an intentional move on the part of his guardian to prove something to him. He'd told Mrs Hawley where they were going for their picnic and she had obviously detailed her husband to lead Lord Evesham and his friends to the lake.

'So there you are!' boomed Lord Evesham as he bore down on the young couple. 'We've come from London in Lord Sunderland's drag.'

Andrew and Eloise scrambled to their feet politely. Lord Evesham said, 'My ward, Lord Drummond. May I introduce Lord Sunderland and Lord Amberley?'

Andrew bowed stiffly as he was introduced to the two men.

'And Miss...?' asked Lord Evesham, raising his hat and standing bald-headed before Eloise.

Lord Evesham knew very well who she was, but for some reason that Andrew could not fathom he wanted to humiliate her. In any case there was no need to introduce Eloise because Mystique, she of the hard, metallic voice that

Andrew hated, rushed towards Eloise with a shriek of recognition.

'Marie!' she cried. 'Why, if it isn't little Marie!'

Then she kissed her. Andrew felt that he could have put his fist in her beautiful mouth. The voice of brass was bad enough, but something told him that this dreadful creature was part of Eloise's wretched past. If an eclipse had come over the sun, the beauty of the day could not have been more spoilt.

The servants, with the dexterity of a conjurer's assistant, unpacked the great basket, spread out a white cloth and, in an instant, a luncheon was served.

Lord Evesham looked at Andrew's spent picnic.

'Ah! I see you've already eaten,' he declared. 'Never mind. Come and sit with us and have a glass.'

There was no gainsaying Lord Evesham when he was in a certain scheming mood. Andrew and Eloise sat down with him and his guests but made no pretence of eating. Eve offered them champagne which they both declined politely.

'Oh, my!' cried Mystique. 'What airs she has! Good champagne, too. Come, Marie. Taste.'

She held out her glass to Eloise, who turned her face away.

'Eloise doesn't drink,' said Andrew. 'Except milk. She is unused to wine.'

Mystique looked at Andrew in disbelief, glass in hand. Then she suddenly laughed in a coarse and raucous way.

'What!' she screamed. 'Not drink? Ah, well. It was different in your modelling days, eh, Marie? Have you given all that up?'

Andrew got to his feet and, as if by some impulse, Eloise rose too.

'I don't know why you choose to call Eloise by the name of Marie,' said Andrew, sternly. 'She does not drink champagne. It is a matter of taste. Were she to do so, I am sure that it would never prompt her to talk and act like a fishwife.'

There was a stunned silence. Even Lord Evesham was at a loss for words, though he smiled indulgently. With Eloise on his arm Andrew walked away from the lake. As he did so he heard the shrill laugh of that awful woman. She called out something that he didn't hear, for Eloise was crying.

'Forget them,' said Andrew, putting his arm round her shoulder.

'It's not them,' Eloise sobbed. 'It's...'

She never finished what she wanted to say but Andrew knew quite well what she meant. It was the past that she was thinking of. Whatever Eloise might have done in the past before Andrew found her it was no longer part of their world.

'Forget it,' Andrew urged again. 'It's a bad dream. Those people aren't real. They don't mean anything. Only my guardian is real and I will speak to him when I get home.'

Andrew dried the girl's eyes with his handkerchief. She smiled through her tears and they made their way back to the house, followed by the rustle of the wind in the leaves and the song of the wood doves.

Andrew advised Mrs Hawley to put Eloise to bed for a while so that she could rest and recover from her unpleasant experience. As he said goodbye to Eloise she pleaded, 'Come and see me again, Andy. Please.'

'Of course,' Andrew assured her.

As Benson drove Andrew away, he said, 'I see you had company, my lord.'

'Yes.' That was all Andrew had to say and the journey was otherwise conducted in silence.

Later that evening Andrew talked to his guardian in the smoking room. He found it very difficult to be angry because Lord Evesham was so pleasant and charming, a gift that he frequently made use of.

'That was a dirty trick you played on me today,' Andrew began.

'Salutary, perhaps,' said Eve. 'Dirty, no.'

'Is Mystique a friend of yours?'

'Spare me!'

'How did she get there, then?'

'You must ask Lord Sutherland. I believe she is his mistress.'

'How can he put up with that dreadful laugh?'

'Fortunately he is quite deaf.'

'If such a person is his mistress, shouldn't he be ostracised from society as you are so afraid that I might be?'

'No.'

'Why not?'

'He is still faithful to his wife.'

'Faithful?'

'According to the tenets of society.'

'Strange society,' muttered Andrew.

'You will learn.'

'Not so long ago you were complimenting Eloise on her beauty, her grace, her modesty.'

'I still do.'

'Then why...?'

'I'm concerned about the future, Andrew. You offer the young lady a home. You provide for her. Your intentions are absolutely honourable, yet you do not love her. That is fine. But it is somewhat strange in the eyes of the world. I, myself, understand, I think. You are a young man of heart and honour, as your father was. Eloise, so to speak, is an old friend, but what is she thinking? Does she love you? She obviously thinks you are a knight in shining armour because of what you've done for her. How is it going to end? Tell me.'

'Why should it end?'

'All right, then. How will it progress?'

'It will stay as it is, as far as I'm concerned. In any case, I don't see how setting Mystique on her helped. It only served to remind her of her past wretchedness.'

'Some of which was optional on her part.'

'No!' exclaimed Andrew heatedly. 'Certainly not!'

'No?' echoed Lord Evesham, calmly.

'No. Pure necessity. Though Mystique tried to make out that she was no better than she should be.'

'She recognised a fellow sufferer.'

'I doubt if Mystique has suffered as Eloise has.'

'You may be right. She has always managed to find a protector.'

'Eloise had no protector until I came along.'

'Andrew, she is not a child. She is not the little girl that you remember. It is in the nature of a woman to love and be loved, to be part of life. Picking violets in the woods at Riverside Towers is not part of that life. I am not entirely destitute of the gift of appreciation. The poetry in life is not dead to me. I can see the poetry in your idyllic relationship. Two young people playing at childhood, refusing to grow up and face life.'

'That's not true.'

'What is true? What is true, Andrew, is that you are getting yourself into a position from which you will not be able to escape with honour.'

'Why?'

'Even if you did wish to marry her . . .'

'Which I don't,' Andrew interrupted.

'Even if you did wish to marry her,' Lord Evesham insisted, 'Society would not accept her as your wife.'

'Why not?'

'That you have got to learn. Obviously.'

'I have no wish to marry Eloise, nor does she wish to marry me. I found her in dire circumstances and rescued her. Have your friends so little heart that they must sneer at something that is natural and good? What is the barrier that divides a man from a woman so that friendship is impossible for them?'

Lord Evesham stood up and prepared to leave the room.

'In a word, dear boy, sex.'

With that he strode out of the room in his usual dignified manner. Andrew still did not understand his motive in invading the picnic, unless it was to show him the kind of people Eloise had been associating with, all of which Andrew knew or could guess. So he had really wasted his time in trying to talk his guardian into accepting Eloise. He hadn't changed his mind, which was wholly occupied with what people in society might think and thus spoil his dilettante existence.

Andrew returned to his own quarters, still determined to help Eloise and Franz, the pillars of his childhood memories.

Franz, indeed, was the next problem. He had been traced to several lodgings, but each time Andrew went to find him the man had moved on. Andrew knew that Franz was a veritable wandering minstrel and that he might not even be in London, though he had told him that their travelling band had broken up.

At length Franz was traced to a depressing house in a very poor quarter of London, and when Andrew called at his lodgings the sound of the violin led him up the dingy, bare stairs. Andrew found him sitting on the side of an iron-framed bed playing something that was quite new to him. Franz was more shocked than surprised to see him.

'How did you find me?' he asked.

'Through the Empress Hall,' Andrew told him. 'But the chase led me all over London. I began to think you'd joined another travelling group.'

'Now that you have found me, my lord, what can I do for you? You want me to play at one of your receptions?'

'No,' said Andrew. 'I was wondering if you would like a day in the country?'

'A day in the country? I had forgotten that such a place existed.'

'Come with me now,' urged Andrew.

Franz did not know what to say. He stared at Andrew, blankly.

'Now?' he asked, vaguely.

'Yes,' said Andrew. 'Come along. I mean it. I want to take you for a drive in the country.'

Franz got off the bed, picked up his hat, put his violin in its battered case and stood before Andrew like a child asking what it should do next.

'Will we be long?' he asked.

'Do you need your violin?' Andrew suggested.

'It never leaves me,' explained Franz, giving the instrument a little pat as he tucked it under his arm.

As they made their way down the rickety stairs Andrew asked, 'Don't you lock your door?"

'There's nothing to steal.'

In the street Benson was waiting with the carriage. He opened the door for Franz.

'Yours?' Franz asked, as he sat down.

'Yes,' said Andrew.

'Very nice.'

The experience seemed to shock him. He had never been in a carriage before. To Franz, even an omnibus was luxury. The carriage no doubt offended his independence, for he looked rather crestfallen as he sat opposite Andrew. When they arrived at Riverside Towers he asked, 'Where is this?'

'It's my country house,' Andrew said.

Franz gave a little chuckle. 'What it is to be rich,' he exclaimed, without any sense of envy or accusation.

As they alighted from the carriage Andrew said, 'There's someone I want you to meet, Franz.

They walked through the house and onto the terrace where Eloise was sitting, sewing a dress. She sprang up when she saw Andrew and hurried to him.

'Andy!' she cried. 'What a lovely surprise.'

She was about to fling her arms round him when she saw that he was not alone.

Andrew wondered if Eloise would remember the episode on the stairs at Ashley Castle.

'Eloise,' said Andrew, by way of introduction. 'Do you know who this is?'

'I . . . No. I don't think so,' she answered.

'Do you remember peeping through the banisters at the musicians at Ashley Castle?'

'Why, yes!'

'This is Franz who looked up but didn't give us away.'

Franz bowed. It was obvious that he regarded Eloise as a beautiful and gracious goddess. His simple soul was already worshipping her as he watched her every movement.

They had lunch under a great chestnut tree that was just preparing to light its thousand clusters of pink candles. Franz forgot his shyness and told them stories of his wanderings, unconsciously dominating the conversation. Andrew and Eloise listened as children must have listened to the tales of their elders. Yet Franz was still a young man. When he played at Ashley Castle he could not have been more than eighteen himself and that had been only ten years ago. He was now twenty-eight, and Eloise, a little older than Andrew, was twenty-one.

After the stories of his travels, it was inevitable that Franz should take out his violin and play. And how he played! Folk songs, gypsy airs, love songs. Lastly he played the tune that Andrew had heard as he made his way up the stairs to the lodgings. It was a tune of his own, a beautiful, haunting melody.

'What was that?' asked Eloise.

'A little something of my own,' admitted Franz, shyly.

'Why don't you write music?' suggested Andrew.

'My dear friend,' Franz said with a smile, 'I am but second violin in a small, unknown orchestra.'

It was the first time that Andrew had heard Franz talk at all bitterly. For that reason he did not broach the subject again. But that did not prevent him from making plans. He wondered if he could rescue this dear friend from the routine of playing second violin in a second rate orchestra. He could not resist asking, against his will, 'Have you written much music, Franz?'

'Snatches,' Franz answered. 'Songs. Dances.'

'They're written down, are they?'

'Oh, yes.' Then he laughed. 'Somewhere.'

'When I take you back to your lodgings will you try to find them for me?'

'But they are nothing,' insisted Franz.

'Never mind,' said Andrew. 'My guardian is Lord Evesham, and he knows a lot of people. He may even know a music publisher who would publish them.'

'Publish them?'

Andrew saw the sudden light of new hope in Franz's face, a light that quickly vanished again.

'Do not say such things,' said Franz sadly. 'They do not happen. They are not even dreams. The world is a hard place and we are lucky if we manage to live, let alone . . .'

His voice trailed away as, perhaps, even so he might have a

dream. He quickly threw off such a mood and played a gay, happy tune on his violin.

When Andrew and Franz left Eloise, Andrew promised to bring him down again if he was not working. Franz usually worked in the evenings until late and consequently had the day to himself, so it was possible.

When they arrived at the lodgings, Andrew followed Franz up the stairs and helped him search for the manuscript music. Franz found a dusty bundle, blew the dust off it, and looked at it oddly.

'Is that it?' asked Andrew.

'Do you really want it?' Franz asked, apologetically.

'Yes, please,' Andrew assured him.

Franz handed the bundle over with a sigh.

'I'll look after it. Don't worry,' said Andrew.

'I wasn't thinking of that. I hope it doesn't embarrass you.'

'I don't think it will do that.'

When he left him, Andrew was aware that he had left the man rather perplexed. He must have been wondering at all the astonishing things that had happened to him since their chance encounter in the street, that night when Franz had been on his way to play at the students ball: a drive into the country in a beautiful coach, meeting a beautiful girl, a beautiful lunch, everything beautiful. And now...

That night Andrew went with his guardian to the opera. It was a performance of *Don Giovanni* and he sat amidst all the splendour of London society, tier upon tier of beauty and magnificence drawn like moths around the flame of Mozart's genius. As he sat there he couldn't help thinking of Franz and his violin. He seemed a long way away from this, his music of little account compared to Mozart.

Yet when Andrew went to bed that night, the music that pursued him was the haunting melody that Franz had played to him and Eloise under the chestnut tree, not Mozart.

Next morning he asked his guardian, 'Do you know any music publishers, Eve?'

'Know what?' asked Eve, quizzically.

'Nothing,' said Andrew, nonchalantly. 'I only wondered.'

'Don't tell me the opera last night has fired you with inspiration to compose.'

'No,' Andrew chuckled. 'A friend of mine.'

'Eloise has composed something apart from herself, has she?' he asked, cynically.

'No. This is a man called Franz Engelman.'

'Where does he fit in?'

'He was playing at Ashley Castle when we were there.'

'That damned place!' exclaimed Eve with feeling. 'It'll be the death of you, my boy.'

'I want to help him. That's all,' explained Andrew, lamely.

'Another one? When are you going to stop?'

'There isn't anyone else.'

'Oh well,' sighed Eve, resignedly. 'The only man I know in the music publishing world is Herman Dravenski. You could try him.'

'Where would I find him?'

'He has offices in Covent Garden.'

'Would you give me a letter of introduction? Please.'

'Of course.'

Lord Evesham got up and went to his secretaire and penned a letter for Andrew to present to Mr Dravenski.

Not wishing to waste time Andrew tucked the manuscript music under his arm and called on Mr Dravenski. It was not easy to get to him. He was protected by so many secretaries and assistants.

Andrew sat patiently in an outer office while his letter of introduction was taken into the great man. At length a somewhat formidable lady in rimless glasses came out of his office and invited Andrew to enter.

Mr Dravenski was a small, round man with a white, fat face out of which protruded a large cigar. He was not tall even when he stood up to greet Andrew. As he shook hands Andrew noticed his clean, white hands and felt the pressure of several rings on his fingers.

'So you're Eve's ward,' he beamed.

Andrew presumed that he must be quite friendly with his guardian to call him Eve.

'A wonderful man,' he went on. 'Full of humour.'

'He certainly is,' agreed Andrew.

'I never met your father, Lord Drummond.'

'No,' said Andrew. 'They didn't meet very often. My father was more of a country man.'

'I see.'

There was a silence between them as Mr Dravenski sat at his huge, ornamental desk.

'What can I do for you, young man?' asked Mr Dravenski eventually.

'There is a musician I know...' Andrew began.

'And he's written something,' prompted Mr Dravenski.

'Well, yes,' admitted Andrew, lamely, handing over the manuscript.

Mr Dravenski chuckled to himself. 'It happens all the time, Lord Drummond,' he explained. 'If I listened to everybody who writes a tune I'd never get any sleep.'

'This is different,' said Andrew.

'It always is.'

'I would like you to see this man, Franz Engelman, and tell him that you will publish his music and pay him what you usually pay. I will then reimburse you. But I don't want him to know what I've done.'

'Oh,' exclaimed Mr Dravenski, subdued.

'Will you do that for me, Mr Dravenski?'

'If you wish me to, Lord Drummond.'

'It will make someone very happy.'

'I won't ask any questions. It's your business what you do with your money. I can only say that it's a very generous gesture and not only unusual but without precedent.'

'It is my pleasure.'

'What will you do? Send him in to me?'

'Yes. He's a violinist and works for a small orchestra that plays for dances.'

'I understand. I'll tell my people to expect him.'

Andrew was aware as he left Mr Dravenski that the man regarded him as something of an eccentric and would no doubt express as much to Lord Evesham when he next met him.

His next call was on Franz at his lodgings. Franz was in bed asleep after a late night playing at some function. Andrew knocked on his door, and it was some time before a tousle-haired man in a nightshirt opened it.

'Oh, it's you, my lord,' he said sleepily.

He opened the door wide to let Andrew enter the room.

'Good morning, Franz,' cried Andrew, cheerily.

'I'm sorry,' said Franz. 'We had a late engagement last night.'

'That's all right, Franz. I'm sorry to disturb you.'

Franz sat on the side of the bed scratching his head and yawning. Andrew sat on the only chair, a rickety upright.

'Does the name Herman Dravenski mean anything to you, Franz?' Andrew asked.

'Of course it does,' replied Franz. 'The biggest music publisher in the business.'

'I've just left there.'

'Oh, yes?'

Franz was not really awake and was not taking a lot of notice of what Andrew was saying.

'I took your music to show Mr Dravenski.'

'Where is it?' asked Franz, suddenly interested in the fate of his 'child'. 'What have you done with it?' He could see that Andrew was not carrying the manuscript to return to him.

'I left it with Mr Dravenski.'

'Why?' Franz asked, almost accusingly.

'Wake up, Franz,' chided Andrew. 'He likes your music and wants to talk to you.'

It wasn't exactly true. But he remembered that when Mr Dravenski looked at the music he had not exactly been put off, though his enthusiasm was muted. Franz was wide awake now.

'What?' he asked, in disbelief. 'Liked it, did you say?'

'He wants you to call and see him,' said Andrew.

'Why?'

'Why do you think? He likes your music and wants to talk to you about publishing it.'

68

Although Franz was now wide awake he was dazed by what Andrew had told him.

'You mean . . . ?' Franz asked in a bemused manner.

Andrew began to be a little impatient with his violinist friend.

'Mr Dravenski can't publish your music without your permission or without talking to you about it,' he explained. 'So I suggest you dress yourself and get round there as soon as possible.'

'Yes. Yes. I will. I will.'

Franz was suddenly galvanised into action. He got off the bed and started busying himself with the business of washing and dressing. Rather than embarrass him, Andrew decided to leave.

'Come and see me at Walpole House afterwards, will you?' Andrew suggested.

'Walpole House?'

'My guardian's house in the park.'

'I'll find it. Yes. Yes.'

'We'll talk then.'

'Yes. Yes.'

Franz wasn't really listening. He was too eager to get dressed and see Mr Dravenski.

It was a very different Franz Engelman who was announced at the magnificent Walpole House later that afternoon. He was wreathed in smiles and near to tears. He fell on his knees in front of Andrew, grabbed his hands and smothered them in kisses.

'How can I thank you?' he cried, tearfully.

'Get up, Franz,' commanded Andrew, sternly. 'Don't be an idiot.'

Franz scrambled to his feet, sheepishly.

'How can I thank you?' he repeated.

'Don't thank me,' said Andrew. 'You wrote the music. I didn't.'

'He bought them!' cried Franz. 'He bought them! I'm rich!'

'Well done,' said Andrew.

69

Once Andrew had calmed Franz down and settled him in a comfortable chair to stop his excited pacing up and down the room, he tried to talk to him about the future. In his own mind he had decided that it would not be practicable to buy everything that Franz wrote from now on, but he could install him in the cottage attached to Riverside Towers where he could work in peace and quiet. Certainly Franz could now leave that depressing hovel that he lived in at present. But if Mr Dravenski's doubts proved correct and the music didn't sell, then Franz would be living in a fool's paradise. Andrew wondered if perhaps he shouldn't defer suggesting such a drastic move as Franz giving up his position in the orchestra and living in the cottage.

'What do you want to do now?' Andrew asked, tentatively.

'Find somewhere to live,' replied Franz, promptly, eagerly.

'You'll stay with the orchestra, will you?'

'Oh, no!' laughed Franz. 'Once I get my foot on the ladder with Mr Dravenski, I want to keep climbing. I'll leave that lot.'

Andrew knew a moment of anxiety, yet he persisted.

'You can stay in my cottage by the river if you like,' he said.

'You mean where that lovely girl lives?'

'No. She lives in the house. The cottage is on the river, lower down.'

'You mean I could . . . ?' Franz was too overcome to go on.

'You could write your music there.'

'I could, couldn't I ?'

Tears came into his eyes again as he smiled beamingly at Andrew, his young benefactor.

'I've never met anybody as kind as you, sir,' he stammered.

'I'm only trying to help,' said Andrew lamely.

'Help!' cried Franz. 'It's more than that. You've saved my life.'

Franz returned to his lodgings and while he was organising his affairs Benson drove Andrew down to Riverside Towers, where he was met a little sulkily by Eloise.

'I thought you'd deserted me,' she complained.

'Never,' said Andrew. 'Wait till I tell you what I've been doing.'

Andrew took her hand and led her down to the cottage by the river. On the way he told her about his visit to the music publisher and his talk with Franz. He told her of Franz's eagerness to work in the cottage. He did not tell her that he was paying Mr Dravenski to publish Franz's music.

'Won't it be lonely for him here after London?' Eloise asked.

'Is it lonely for you after London?'

Eloise was thoughtful. 'Sometimes,' she admitted, shyly.

'He'll be working,' Andrew explained. 'Writing his music.'

'Not all the time.'

'Then he can come up to the house and keep you company or you can come down here and keep him company.'

'Yes,' said Eloise. 'I'd like that.'

As they stood outside the cottage Eloise ventured out onto the jetty that had served as a mooring for a boat which did not exist at present.

'Be careful, Eloise,' cried Andrew. 'That's not safe. It needs repairing.'

Eloise looked over the rail into the water.

'Are there any fish?' she asked.

'I don't think so.'

'I thought I saw one. It looked like a face.'

Andrew suddenly remembered the beautiful Carl and the time he fell into the lake at Ashley Castle. He felt sentimental about him. He liked Carl, almost loved him, certainly loved the memory of him. He also felt sorry for him. He couldn't accept that there was any real hatred between them. On the landing at the castle when they were listening to the music there had been a tenderness between them.

'You made me think of Carl when you talked about a face,' Andrew told Eloise.

Eloise came cautiously back onto dry land and stood beside Andrew. 'I wonder what she's doing now,' she said.

'Who?' asked Andrew, puzzled.

'Carl.'

'You said "she".'

'I know.'

Andrew laughed. He still couldn't accept Eloise's theory that Carl was a girl. It was typical of Eloise's capricious nature to persist in it, a childish myth. Andrew had to admit that he would prefer Carl to be a girl for he was indeed beautiful.

Andrew returned with Eloise to the house and when it came to say goodbye, she kissed him on the lips. She threw her arms round his neck and pulled him down to her. His reaction was to hold her gently. He did not return the kiss.

'Dear Andy,' murmured Eloise, dreamily, with her eyes shut. 'I love you.'

Andrew chuckled in his embarrassment. 'Eloise...' he murmured.

'I couldn't bear it if I didn't see you,' she went on. 'You are my life. Don't ever leave me, please.'

'I'm not likely to do that,' said Andrew, not really knowing what to say.

That kiss worried him all the way home. It was just as though a dark cloud had appeared on his otherwise sunny horizon, a cloud no larger than Eloise's small hand, but a cloud nevertheless. Andrew did not love her. At least, not in the way she might have wanted. He was very fond of her, more than fond, otherwise he wouldn't have installed her in Riverside Towers. He did not want to be unkind or heartless where she was concerned, but he had to make her understand how he felt and he didn't know how to go about it. He couldn't take it for granted that she loved him in the way he imagined, but they had never kissed before and he was sure that Eloise would never have made the gesture, which was a sign of her feelings, just for the sake of decorum.

Was Lord Evesham's warning coming true, Andrew wondered. Had he embarked on a dangerous mission, emotionally, in trying to help people? Eve had asked how it would end. Was he expected to marry Eloise? Is that what she was hoping for? How could he marry someone he didn't love? No doubt many marriages had succeeded on the basis of mere fondness but he hoped to avoid such a situation.

What did it mean, that kiss? Was Eloise expecting something more than friendship? Had he misled her? If not marriage, did she expect him to make her his mistress? That was completely out of the question. Had he compromised her by setting her up in Riverside Towers? Was he under some obligation to her? What was she expecting of him? She had made her feelings quite obvious with that kiss, feelings which he could not reciprocate. So it was down to duty. Was it is his duty to marry her? Taking her away from the students' ball and taking her away from her dingy lodgings must have given her the impression that he was doing it for some selfish motive, as if she belonged to him – so that's what she thought, that she belonged to him? In that case he was certainly under an obligation either to end the whole business or take it further, which would mean marriage. He couldn't let her go back to that old life. That would be unfair, unkind. The alternative, apart from marriage, was to let her stay at Riverside Towers on her own, devoid of male company, devoid of any prospect of marriage, an exile.

At home at Walpole House Andrew was often to be found by the lakeside gazing into the water. Water attracted him and it never failed to remind him of Carl. One day he was joined by his guardian, who very rarely ventured so far away from the comfort of his winged armchair.

'What's worrying you, Andrew?' Eve asked.

Andrew looked round in surprise. He had not heard his guardian approaching.

'You haven't been your normal self lately, my boy. What's worrying you?'

'Nothing,' declared Andrew. 'Nothing's worrying me.'

'Have you got yourself into a muddle with that girl?'

Andrew was amazed at the old man's perception.

'Something has gone wrong,' Eve persisted. 'I can tell.'

'No,' Andrew asserted. 'Nothing's gone wrong.'

'You know you could never marry her, don't you?'

'Why not?' demanded Andrew.

'She would never be accepted by society as your wife. As something else, perhaps. But not a wife.'

Andrew swallowed the insult to Eloise in his guardian's remark.

'I have no wish to marry her,' said Andrew.

'Then what is the trouble?'

'I think she may expect me to.'

'Oh dear.'

That just about summed up the situation, thought Andrew: Oh dear. A new era of life had begun for him. The truth of Lord Evesham's philosophy was borne in upon him. What was he to do about Eloise? A more experienced man of the world would have known, but Andrew was not that man. All he could do was stay away from Riverside Towers for a while. At least until it was time for the installation of Franz Engelman.

'Oh dear,' sighed Lord Evesham again and walked back to the house.

Andrew was left alone.

Eloise was blissfully unaware of the turmoil going on in Andrew's mind as she sat at her sewing. She was certainly not thinking of marriage either to Andrew or anyone. Her feelings for Andrew were heartfelt and sincere. It was his kindness she admired as much as the man himself. If anything happened to him she would be heartbroken, such was the measure of her affection. She could never imagine any physical contact with him apart from wanting to kiss him out of gratitude. Even during her years of modelling, in spite of what people may have thought, she had always avoided physical contact with artists, no matter what the artists themselves might have boasted. She was, in fact, still a virgin. She was happy. That was all she knew and the man who had made her happy was Andrew.

When he left Andrew by the lake Lord Evesham decided that he should take a hand in the affair and visit the girl himself. He would explain to her, as tactfully as possible, the obligations that his ward, Andrew, owed to Society and her place in the order of things. Andrew had no idea that his guardian was contemplating such a move, so when he learned that Lord Evesham had gone out in his carriage he presumed that he was visiting one of his Society friends.

As Lord Evesham's carriage arrived at Riverside Towers, he was greeted by old Hawley.

'Is Miss Ashley at home?' asked Eve.

'Yes, sir,' said Hawley. 'May I ask who is calling?'

'Lord Evesham.'

Hawley left Lord Evesham in the vaulted hall while he went to inform Eloise.

'Lord Evesham has called to see you, Miss,' he announced.

'Lord Evesham?' said Eloise, in surprise. The announcement sounded ominous to her for some unknown reason.

'He is waiting in the hall, Miss,' Hawley prompted.

'Show him in,' she said at last, still puzzled and worried.

As Hawley left the room, she stood up and brushed her hands over her dress and hair and waited to receive Andrew's guardian.

When he came into the room she was impressed by his impeccable appearance, his dignity, his air of authority.

'Lord Evesham,' she cried, 'what an unexpected pleasure.'

'My dear lady, how attractive you look,' fawned the old man.

'Thank you. Won't you sit down?'

They sat in comfortable armchairs facing each other.

'I'm sorry to take you by surprise,' Lord Evesham began, 'but I couldn't wait to advise you of my visit as I considered my errand somewhat urgent.'

'Oh,' breathed Eloise. 'Is it something to do with Andrew?'

'Yes.'

'He is not ill, is he?' she asked, nervously.

'No. I wanted to explain something to you.'

'About him?'

'Yes.'

'Please do.'

Lord Evesham hesitated. Then he plunged on, disconcerted by the girl's composure.

'Andrew is coming to an age when you might expect a man to think of taking a wife.'

'He's not getting married, is he?'

'What would you say if he was?'

'I'd say I think he might have told me.'

'Why?'

'So that I could congratulate him.'

'Is that all?'

'Also wish him the best of luck and so on,' Eloise added, lightly.

Lord Evesham regarded her closely, trying to discover if she was telling the truth. If, in fact, such news would not have devastated her.

'You wouldn't mind?'

'No. I'd be a little hurt, of course.'

'Oh? Why?'

'Because he didn't tell me.'

'Not because you might want him to marry him yourself?'

'No. I've never thought of Andrew in that way.'

'You haven't?'

'No. He's a dear friend. He's an angel. He's helped me enormously. I'll always be grateful to him. But if all this came to an end...'

She made a gesture with her hands that embraced the whole of Riverside Towers. She shrugged her shoulders. 'I suppose I could always go back to work,' she concluded.

'Why should it end?' asked Lord Evesham.

'If he gets married he wouldn't want to keep me here.'

'Why not?'

'It wouldn't look right. Besides, he might want to live here with his wife.'

Lord Evesham gave a little laugh. 'It's not likely to end yet, my dear.'

'Oh, Andrew is a saint,' Eloise cried. 'I can tell you that.'

'Some people might consider him foolhardy.'

'I expect so. People like the friends you brought down that day when we were having a picnic in the woods.'

'Exactly.'

Lord Evesham accepted the gentle rebuff. This girl was no idiot, he decided. He had come to warn her that she could never marry his ward, and here she was making it quite clear that such was neither her intention nor her hope. Andrew had got hold of the wrong end of the stick. But how could he? Young as he was, he should know the signs. Lord Evesham himself had come out to Riverside Towers prepared to argue with this delicate creature and here she was practically agreeing with him. Whether she was hiding her real feelings or not he could not tell. He now had the embarrassing task of extricating himself from the predicament that was of his own creation. He couldn't tell her the real reason for his calling, namely to make her understand that, as the wife of Andrew, she would be socially unacceptable. It would be cruel now to suggest such a thing.

'You said your visit was urgent, Lord Evesham. What is the urgency?' Eloise asked, disarmingly.

'I wanted to warn you of the possibility of Andrew marrying,' Lord Evesham admitted lamely.

'Who is the lucky lady?'

'Oh, there is nobody at the moment.'

'There isn't?'

'No.'

'Then there's no urgency.'

There was a brief silence between them.

'Is there?' she insisted.

'Perhaps not,' admitted Lord Evesham, grudgingly.

'Unless, of course,' Eloise went on, 'you thought I might have designs on him myself.'

'No. No,' denied Lord Evesham, aware of his own hypocrisy. 'But you did embrace him rather lovingly the other day, didn't you?'

Eloise blushed.

'He told you that, did he? Does he tell you everything?'

'Only things that worry him.'

'Poor Andrew. He's so innocent. I admit I was carried away by his generosity to Franz.'

She gave a little laugh and stood up as a signal that she no longer wished to continue the conversation.

'I would like you to excuse me now, Lord Evesham,' she said.

'Of course. Thank you for receiving me.'

'Give my kind regards to Lord Sunderland and the ladies.'

'I certainly will.'

Andrew stayed away from Riverside Towers until it was time to install Franz Engelman in the cottage by the river. Franz brought his luggage with him, done up in a brown paper parcel and, of course, his beloved violin. He looked the real Bohemian. Besides his meagre luggage and his violin, he was carrying some rolls of music paper.

His eyes lit up when he saw that Andrew had moved a piano into the cottage. It seemed that anything to do with music, be it sight or sound, made him happy.

Eloise watched Andrew warily, wishing to avoid any embarrassment to him, particularly in front of Franz. For his part Andrew seemed rather shy of her. All three of them had tea in the drawing room and Eloise offered to help Franz move into the cottage. Franz was too overcome with excitement to do anything but let the waves of happiness envelop him.

When Andrew left them Eloise was careful to kiss him only on the cheek in a sisterly fashion, a gesture he was not slow to appreciate.

'You see?' she said.

'See what?'

'I only kiss you on the cheek in future.'

'Oh. Why is that?'

'I don't want to frighten you.'

They laughed as they parted, though Andrew felt guilty.

As the summer went on Andrew was taken by Lord Evesham to dinners, balls and receptions. Because he was young and good looking and was known to be quite wealthy he was well received. The summer seemed to be one continual round of parties and people.

At Riverside Towers Franz was lost in his music in the paradise in which he now found himself. He seemed to have recovered the years of his youth. His genius, held back for so long, suddenly burst forth. He was projecting and working on a great opus, an opera founded on some old legend. To add to his joy, Herman Dravenski, the music publisher, had discovered that the music that Andrew had paid him to publish had turned out to be quite successful. Andrew was paid back his own money and Mr Dravenski developed a healthy respect for Franz. So all was well with the little violinist.

But not so with Eloise. At first Andrew thought it was his fancy, but by midsummer he was certain. Franz was a frequent visitor to Riverside Towers and would wander up from the cottage to chat to Eloise. When he was there Eloise seemed bright and gay, which could have been the effect of bravado because when she was alone she was abstracted and sad. Her cheeks had lost their colour and Mrs Hawley, the housekeeper, said she wasn't eating properly. The meaning was plain. But the signs that would have given a lover joy filled Andrew with anxiety. He had offered her protection. The natural sequence of events of course, would be for him to marry her. But if he married her, then society, according to Lord Evesham, would not receive her as his wife. What did Andrew care for society? To what extent could he play the rebel? He had his own family name to think of apart from that of his guardian's. Everybody could become tainted as Eloise had become tainted through no fault of her own, for on top of her father's financial disgrace, there was her so-called dubious career as an artist's model. If Andrew had loved her, he would have cared little for society, but he didn't love her. He even experienced a feeling of panic whenever the idea of marriage came into his mind. He had his whole life before him, and if he married Eloise he would be tied to a woman he didn't love. Fond, yes. Sympathetic, yes. And what would happen then if he fell in love with somebody else? Had he made Eloise love him by helping her? In that case he must ask her to be his wife, for under the guise of brotherly friendship he had virtually designated her his lover. Of course, he could make her his mistress. But would that be fair? Or he could marry her and take a mistress to himself when he later fell in love, but he never thought that those arrangements were very satisfactory. He had already noticed that the husband who took a mistress had little feeling for his wife. In any case, that would not be fair to the mistress if they were both in love.

After his last visit to Riverside Towers, Andrew returned to London with his mind made up. He would marry Eloise. She was obviously unhappy. He would tell his guardian before he told her.

He confronted Lord Evesham in his library.'

'Eve,' he began. 'I've decided to take the fatal step.'

'What step is that, dear boy?'

'You told me that I was getting myself into a difficult situation.

'And you are?'

'Yes.'

Andrew then told his guardian of his struggle with his conscience and his decision to ask Eloise to marry him. Then there was silence.

'You don't seem surprised,' said Andrew.

'The only thing that would have surprised me would have been if all this hadn't occurred. You know, of course, that it will mean social ruin and, as you say you don't love the girl, the ruin of any chance of your own happiness.'

'I'm aware of that.'

'I'm getting old, Andrew,' admitted the old man. 'I have no children. I looked upon you as if you were my own child. I had plans for your future, a magnificent future. I took pleasure in introducing you to my friends, in seeing you well received. You could have been a great figure, a great success in Society. And now, in a moment, all that can vanish. You must excuse me if I complain, Andrew. Your own suicide would sadden me less than such a marriage. You are a man and it is not for me to treat you as though you were a child. I suggest you take the advice of your pillow and sleep on it.'

'Very well,' agreed Andrew. 'I'll do that but I doubt if it will change my mind.'

As Andrew went out of the room Lord Evesham wondered if anything had happened between the two young people since his interview with Eloise. She had said that she had no design on Andrew. He could not be certain that her protestation of indifference would survive once Andrew proposed. At that time he had not proposed, he simply felt that she was in love with him, a feeling prompted by his generosity towards her. It was the kiss that had put the idea into his head. Considering the girl's past, it was not unlikely that such an embrace was common currency among her associates. Lord Evesham dared not approach Eloise again and he dared not tell Andrew of his interview with her. He could only hope that when Andrew proposed, she turned him down, and until that happened he would be living in suspense.

As Andrew approached Riverside Towers, he wondered what he was going to say to Eloise. How could he lead up to asking her to marry him?

Eloise led him onto the terrace where they sat on a raffia sofa covered with floral cushions.

'It's a long time since you came to see me, Andy,' she said.

'Oh, that's Eve's fault,' said Andrew. 'He's kept me at it. Receptions, balls, dinners, opera. He's exhausted me. I don't know how he does it himself.'

'He hasn't anything else to do, has he?'

'Well, no. I suppose not.'

'He can sleep all day if he wants to.'

'So could I, I suppose. But I don't want that kind of life.'

'I shouldn't think so.'

'Do you miss parties and dancing, Eloise?'

'No. I'm all for the quiet life now.'

'But you're too young to shut yourself away.'

'I prefer it at the moment.'

'Don't you get lonely?'

'I look forward to you coming. But now that Franz is here, there's someone to talk to.' She gave a little laugh. 'When he's not up to his ears in his music, of course.'

'So you don't miss me so much now?' suggested Andrew.

'I will always miss you, Andy. You know that. You're very special to me.'

'Would you like me to live here permanently instead of in London?'

'Could you? That would be wonderful.'

Eloise could not conceal her excitement which Andrew was not slow to notice.

'I wouldn't want to compromise you.'

'How would you do that?'

'Well . . .' Andrew hesitated. 'We'd have to be married.'

'Oh.' Eloise's disappointment was obvious.

'Would you marry me, Eloise?'

'Are you asking me?'

'Well . . . Yes.'

'I don't know what to say.'

'You can only say yes or no. Or do you want time to think about it? I've been rather abrupt, I know.'

'No. No. It's not that. I love you very much, Andy. I always will. More than I can say. More than you can know. But . . .' Eloise avoided looking at Andrew and tears came into her eyes. She dabbed at her eyes with her little handkerchief.

'Oh, Eloise,' cried Andrew. 'Don't cry. Please. I didn't mean to upset you.'

Eloise shook her head. 'I'm so sorry,' she sobbed.

Andrew put his arms round her shoulder but she shrugged them away and stood up suddenly.

'No. No. Don't touch me,' she cried.

Andrew stood up. 'Oh, God! What have I done?'

Eloise turned and faced him. 'I can't marry you, Andrew,' she said, firmly.

'Oh. I see.'

Andrew sat down again. He wanted to ask why Eloise couldn't marry him, but as he was asking out of what he thought was his duty, he wondered if it was wise to pursue the subject at all now. Eloise sat beside him again, more composed.

'I can't explain, Andy,' she said, using the familiar name once again. 'It's just . . . I've never thought of us like that.'

'I understand,' said Andrew.

'I don't think you do, but it won't make any difference between us, will it?'

'No. No. Certainly not,' Andrew assured her.

Eloise escorted Andrew to the front door and saw him into his coach after embracing him in a friendly fashion. She waved her sodden handkerchief as he drove away. He leaned out of the window and waved until he was out of sight.

Eloise turned sadly and returned to the house. She sat once again on the terrace sofa and simply stared into space. She had never considered the subject of marriage with anybody, least of all Andrew. Had Andrew's proposal any connection with Lord Evesham's visit, she wondered. That old gentleman had seemed rather concerned that she might wish to marry his ward, since he had avoided connecting the two of them together in his conversation but vaguely alluded to some anonymous lady. Eloise was quite convinced that there was no such person and could only assume that Lord Evesham was trying to give her some kind of warning not to prejudice such a hypothetical possibility. He was, in fact, trying to say that she was not good enough for Andrew. The exhibition at the picnic had told her that much. There could be no doubt that the introduction of Mystique, a notorious model if ever there was one, was designed to remind Andrew that he was attaching himself to someone who, in spite of her aristocratic lineage, might not be accepted by Society. Or was Lord Evesham trying to tell her that she should not accept Andrew's generosity without some recompense? Yet how could she do that? She would marry Andrew if he insisted, if it was a matter of life or death, but she doubted if such a marriage would bring anything but social ostracism to her dear Andrew. In any case, Andrew had never shown any sign of actually being in love with her. They had never behaved like lovers, had never touched each other that way. Yet Andrew had suddenly asked her to marry him. Did he feel under some kind of obligation because he had installed her in Riverside Towers? Was he trying to save her good name and in so doing destroy his own?

She decided that there must be a part of Andrew that she didn't understand. He certainly didn't appear disappointed that she had not accepted his proposal. He was sorry that he might have upset her, but that was all. One day she would ask him what prompted his action. But not now.

In the carriage on his way back to London Andrew could not but feel sorry for Eloise. His sadness could almost turn to love, but he knew that his original feelings had not changed.

Other people's tears upset him and he wanted to comfort them. He could not understand what had made Eloise cry. She had said that she couldn't marry him, not that she wouldn't. What did that mean? Was it anything to do with Lord Evesham's interruption of their picnic that day? Perhaps when they met again in less emotional circumstances, she would tell him why she refused him.

It was only a few days after his return to London that Benson told him that he had a visitor.

'Who is it?'

'That violinist fellow,' said Benson, without enthusiasm.

'You mean Franz Engelman, the composer,' Andrew chided his servant.

'As you say, my lord,' said Benson.

'Well, show him up,' urged Andrew.

Benson hurried out of the room, and when Franz appeared, he simply stood in the doorway, arms outstretched and a seraphic smile on his face.

'Behold!' he cried.

'Behold what?' asked Andrew tolerantly.

'My angel loves me!' announced Franz.

Who Franz's angel was Andrew had no idea, but whoever it was had made the man very happy. He looked quite radiant and laughed like a boy.

'How did you get here?' asked Andrew. 'You couldn't have walked all that way.'

'I flew. I am walking on air.'

'Well, come down to earth,' advised Andrew. 'And tell me what it's all about.'

'I came by carriage and foot to tell you, to let you be the first to know, that my angel loves me.'

'That's wonderful. But who is this angel?'

Andrew might have been talking to a brick wall, so absorbed was Franz in his news that he couldn't speak. Then he explained.

'Yesterday I was in despair. She had not understood me. She thought I cared for nothing but my music. Little did she know that she was my music, that her whole being, body and soul, had entered into my music, that she . . .'

'Wait! Wait!' Andrew ordered, but he could not quell his friend.

'She did not realise,' Franz went on, enthusiastically, 'that she was me, that my music was her, that every strand of her hair, every motion of her lips . . .'

'Franz!' shouted Andrew. 'Who are you talking about?'

Franz was suddenly silent, as if in shock. Then he said very quietly, 'Eloise, of course.'

Now it was Andrew's turn to observe a shocked silence. When he recovered, he asked, 'You and Eloise?'

'Yes. Yes. She loves me!'

'Franz!'

They hugged each other. They were both excited, Franz with his requited love and Andrew with relief. Actually, Andrew was so relieved that he could have kissed him, too. He knew that Franz and Eloise would be happy, and he realised now why she had behaved as she did when he last saw her. He remembered that when he was alone with Eloise, she was rather sad but was elated whenever Franz happened to visit from the cottage. Why hadn't he realised it instead of presuming that Eloise was in love with him? It was that passionate kiss, of course, that had fooled him. It was a passion she wanted to release and he was the only convenient person she could trust. There was a cynical bitterness in the recollection, for he had been on the verge of what Lord Evesham would consider sacrificing himself on the altar of Pity.

Andrew wanted his guardian to know the news at once so he rang for Benson to bring some wine and, once he had calmed Franz down, asked him to excuse him for a moment.

He hurried to Lord Evesham's quarters, knocked on the door and entered without waiting for a reply. Johnson, his guardian's valet, was tying the old man's cravat. Andrew took the man by the shoulders and marched him out of the room.

'Out, Johnson!' he cried.

'Andrew!' rebuked Lord Evesham.

Andrew leaned against the closed door and gasped, 'We're saved!'

Lord Evesham stood facing Andrew, his striped silk cravat hanging loose, his face angry.

'What the devil are you talking about, boy?' he demanded.

'Eloise.'

'What about her?'

'She wasn't in love with me at all. It was Franz, the musician. He's in my room. He just told me all about it. He's ecstatic.'

'I must say, Andrew, your exuberance is a poor compliment to Eloise.'

Andrew became suddenly subdued, even crestfallen.

'I'm sorry,' he said. 'I didn't mean any slight on Eloise. I'd asked her to marry me and she refused me. I asked her out of duty, you see, and now...

'As you say, you're saved.'

'Yes.'

'You don't have to marry the girl after all.'

'No.'

'Well, Andrew, all I can say is that I hope you don't let the girl know how relieved you are.'

'Of course not. I wouldn't dream of such a thing.'

'You see? You can be a hypocrite when you want to. You'll make your mark in society yet.'

'She didn't say she wouldn't marry me. She said she couldn't.'

Lord Evesham understood the significance of the rejection. The girl could still be in love with the boy, he thought, and after their little interview together at Riverside Towers, Eve had begun to feel sorry for her for the first time. Her father had been killed by Andrew's father, her mother had died in penury due to her own father's nefarious dealings, Eloise had been forced to resort to modelling, had been rescued by the boy she loved and then had been forced to reject his offer of marriage. No doubt she had turned to the man called Franz on the rebound, though he, obviously, was a genuine and enthusiastic suitor.

Lord Evesham asked, 'Is he still with you, this Franz?'

'Yes,' said Andrew. 'I left him in my room. I couldn't wait to tell you the news.'

'I would like to meet him. Ask him to lunch.'

'Well...' Andrew hesitated. 'I mean he's not exactly a man about town. He's a bit of a Bohemian.'

'My dear boy, when the house is on fire you don't question the colour of the horses pulling the fire engine. Ask him to lunch even if he's dressed as a Red Indian. You owe him that much for your deliverance.'

When Andrew left his guardian he did not feel very proud of himself. He shouldn't have been quite so excited about the news. Of course his reaction was an unfair reflection on Eloise. He realised that now. She had turned him down, much to his surprise. So why should he react so differently now? He hadn't told his guardian of Eloise's rejection of him. He could have said that he was saved then. It wasn't pride that prevented his mentioning it. It was sadness. He thought she had been unhappy because of him. The very fact that she and Franz loved each other sparked the relief. He was excited for both of them.

Franz, when Andrew entered his room, had not touched the wine or the cigars. He was in a frame of mind far beyond such things. He was standing looking out of the window. Andrew made him sit down, which he found difficult in his restlessness. Andrew sat with him while he listened to the whole story.

Franz said that the idea of loving Eloise had not come of itself. Andrew, as he listened, had to keep reminding himself that the words were coming from a composer and musician and not a normal being, and therefore his language, like that of a poet, was somewhat removed from the normal. Franz evidently considered himself far too humble to worship Eloise, except as one worships the sun or the moon. It was his music that told him that they loved each other, divine love had brought them together. He had loved her without knowing it from the first time they met. When he first told her how he felt, she had run away from him and hid herself in her room. He thought that he had offended her. It wasn't until later in the evening, after he had spent the day in despair, that he saw her seated beneath the giant oak tree in the garden where she had a basket of needlework by her side. In her lap was an old coat of his that she had made him bring to the house for her to mend. He watched her for a moment and then, to his surprise, she held it to her breast and embraced it. Then he knew.

'Ah! My friend,' breathed Franz, in contentment. 'I knew then that all was well with my world. I had come home after all the weary years of travelling.'

Andrew and Franz sat drinking wine with little more to say to each other as Franz repeated his story and expressed his excitement over and over again. Andrew realised again how much he had misunderstood Eloise.

Suddenly, without warning, the door burst open and the cheery voice of Lord Evesham demanded to be introduced to the violinist.

Andrew would never forget the lunch that followed and the kindness of his guardian. The tall footmen who served them might have wondered about the very unaccustomed guest, but if the king himself had been sitting in the place of Franz, then Lord Evesham could not have laid himself out more to please. And from no ulterior motive, no suppressed amusement or condescension. Franz was his guest whom he had invited to lunch. He was not slow to see that the violinist was ill at ease in such strange surroundings, and with the exquisite delicacy found only in a man of noble birth trained in the subtleties of life, he set himself the task of putting his guest at ease.

When the meal was over and the three of them returned to the library, Lord Evesham, for the first time, referred to Eloise. He expressed the wish to give the bride away at the wedding, which delighted both Andrew and Franz.

'We'll give them a good send-off,' said Lord Evesham to Andrew. 'I suggest they get married in Windsor and let Riverside Towers be *en fete* for the occasion.'

Lord Evesham then declared that it was time for his siesta and left the musician and Andrew alone. Andrew wondered a little sadly what Eloise was doing at that moment and how she was feeling. Franz would return to her full of news of Lord Evesham's proposals, but she had not been consulted and Andrew made Franz promise that she would not be bound by such proposals. It would be her day and whatever she wanted would be carried out. As it transpired, Eloise was only too delighted to agree to the proposals.

A few days after the lunch with Franz, Andrew drove to Riverside Towers and walked with Eloise in the gardens.

'You know that I'm very happy for you, don't you, Eloise?' he said.

'Yes,' she replied.

'Do you think you will be happy?'

'Oh, yes.'

'I think your mother would be pleased.'

'Yes. Poor Mother.'

'And Carl. If he knew.'

Eloise gave a little laugh. 'I wonder where he is.'

'It's a pity he can't come to the wedding, your brother.'

'Yes...'

They walked on in silence. When they reached the river Andrew looked into its depth and again recalled the occasion when he had been with Carl at Ashley Castle. When he came out of his brief reverie, he said, 'I must get that jetty repaired. It's dangerous.'

They returned to the house where Franz was waiting for them on the terrace. Andrew looked at Eloise, whose face was radiant.

The wedding took place in the little village church between Windsor and Riverside Towers. Franz had invited one or two of his musician friends, who turned out to be less Bohemian than Franz himself, and between them, in their best clothes, complete with floral buttonholes, they looked like tailor's dummies, but happy.

Eloise had no relatives or friends to invite. She certainly wanted nothing to do with her former modelling acquaintances. Andrew again wished that Carl could witness his sister's marriage. He was the last remaining member of the feuding family and Andrew felt that his presence would further heal the rift between the two families. Whether he would learn of the marriage was hard to tell. Nobody knew where he was. Andrew still had a great fondness for the boy. Boy? They were of a similar age. Carl still cast a spell over him, and whether he was enemy or friend, Andrew could not but wish that they could be together to witness the joining in matrimony of Eloise and Franz.

Lord Evesham walked up the aisle with Eloise on his arm. He, of course, was a picture of aristocratic elegance. She looked ravishing in a simple wedding gown that she had made herself.

At the wedding feast, Lord Evesham was his charming self, insisting on being introduced to every guest, chatting and laughing, suffusing the whole wedding party with his own grace and refinement, causing each person he met to feel elevated and welcome.

Scarcely had they sat down to enjoy the feast than a waiter approached Lord Evesham and whispered something in his ear. His countenance lit up and he said to the waiter, 'Show him in! Show him in!'

Andrew anxiously asked his guardian what that was all about.

'You'll see, my boy,' he replied. 'You'll see.'

To Andrew's great surprise, it was Mr Dravenski, the music publisher, who was shown into the room. He had heard in a roundabout way that the composer, Franz Engelman, was getting married and wanted to impart some important news to him. This news he told first of all to Lord Evesham, who, once a place had been made at the table for the extra guest, took it upon himself to stand up and make a speech.

'Before I toast the health and happiness of the bride and bridegroom, I would like to tell you that I have just learned that the clever groom has written an opera, of all things.'

There was a murmur of both surprise and approval among the guests.

'Rather a rash thing to do, you might say,' Lord Evesham continued, 'but I have sitting beside me a late arrival at this reception, none other than that well known music publisher, Mr Herman Dravenski. He has come here today expressly to inform our composer that his opera has been accepted and will be performed at the . . .'

Before Lord Evesham could say any more the whole company erupted in loud applause, and Éloise, with tears in her eyes, threw her arms compulsively round her husband's neck and kissed him.

When the noise died down sufficiently for Lord Evesham to continue, he said, 'The clever young man is to be congratulated. I am told that the Royal Opera Company will advise him officially in due course, but Mr Dravenski very kindly thought that the good news would add joy to an already joyous occasion.'

Dear, lovable Lord Evesham was applauded loudly as he sat down and the loud buzz of excited conversation filled the room. So, thought Andrew to himself, his faith in Franz had not been misplaced. He was now surely on the road to success and the riches that had for so long eluded him. There was no reason why he and Eloise should not be perfectly happy. There seemed to be no one now for Andrew to help unless, of course, Carl came into his life again.

It was some months after the wedding that one evening Lord Evesham called on Andrew in his quarters and said he wanted to talk. He sat down in a large wing armchair. Andrew had never known him to look so serious and worried.

'Andrew,' he said, 'I want to talk to you about money.'

'You think I'm spending too much?' Andrew asked.

'No. No. You are living well within your means in spite of your generosity. No. I want to talk about all our money, yours and mine.'

Andrew said nothing, wondering what was worrying his guardian.

'I have invested your money as your father intended,' Lord Evesham went on. 'The same investments as mine.

'What is the problem?' asked Andrew.

'Some of those investments are in France, in French companies,' Lord Evesham explained.

'Yes. I've noticed. They've been paying good dividends.'
'Up till now.'
'Oh.'
'I'm worried about France, Andrew. From what I hear, there's going to be trouble there.'
'What kind of trouble?'
'War.'
'What!' Andrew cried in alarm.
'I'm afraid so.'
'How terrible.'
'So I am taking our money out.'
'Very wise.
'I'm glad you agree.'

Before Andrew left the short interview, Lord Evesham reminded him that he was to accompany him that evening to the Duke of Dorset's Ball, one of the great events of the Season. Andrew was not particularly overjoyed at the prospect. Such functions did not appeal to him and dancing even less. The affairs always went on so late, not that that in any way affected Lord Evesham.

Andrew and his guardian dined tête-à-tête prior to the event. At ten o'clock they were told that the carriage was at the door and they left for Lord Dorset's mansion on the other side of the park.

It was a big affair, the Dorset Ball. The whole area about the house was filled with carriages, and Lord Evesham's carriage was wedged between that of Lord Portal and the Russian Ambassador. With time on their hands because of the crush of traffic Lord Evesham took advantage to moan to the Russian Ambassador about France and the possible war.

They eventually arrived at the entrance to Lord Dorset's house. They passed up the wide stairway between a double bank of flowers. The great ballroom was decorated in red and gold. Andrew admired the huge crystal chandeliers in the beautiful ceiling. It could have been the Palace of Versailles. There was an overpowering scent from the banks of camellias and above it all the lively strains of the orchestra.

Andrew was soon separated from his guardian by people

who wanted to speak to the elegant old aristocrat. Lord Evesham would certainly not be dancing. He would spend his time gossiping, which he thoroughly enjoyed. Andrew was on his own and chatting with Dorset's young brother when he saw come into the room a young man, dark and very handsome with an air of distinction which marked him at once as a person above other people, a distinction which reduced the surrounding company to the level of waxwork figures. He was dressed in simple evening attire without jewellery or adornment of any description except an Order set in brilliants on his left breast.

Andrew plucked young Dorset's sleeve. 'That man,' he said, urgently. 'Who is he?'

'That?' replied Dorset. 'Oh, that's the new Lord Ashley. He's the sensation of London at the moment. I'm surprised you haven't heard. His father left a bit of a stink behind financially but this one has lived abroad for years, made a pile and paid off all his father's debts. His father was killed in a duel, by the way.'

'I know,' said Andrew, in a matter-of-fact voice. 'It was a duel with my father.'

'I think duelling should be banned,' declared young Dorset.

'So do I,' agreed Andrew.

The new Lord Ashley, known to Andrew as Carl, looked in his direction, caught his eye and stopped dead in his tracks. He seemed stricken with paralysis. They stared at each other for perhaps ten seconds. It was difficult to tell which of the two was more terrified, shocked. It was as if they had each seen a ghost. Andrew lived again that moment when little Carl had fallen into the lake, and when his father had tried to smother him. It was as if the family tale of the tragedy, told to him by Eloise in the Ashley Castle picture gallery all those years ago, could come to take place again. Andrew felt no animosity towards Carl. He loved him. But he couldn't help feeling that he was not safe in his presence. The tragedy that occurred so long ago, long before either of them was born, when Andrew's lookalike murdered Carl's lookalike in a moment of passion was not likely to repeat itself with Andrew killing Carl, but Carl might want revenge for the death of his father. In memory, Andrew was once more standing in the forest clearing with his father, hearing again the sigh of the wind above the pines, seeing again the blood gushing from the wound in Lord Ashley's breast.

In the silent confrontation, Andrew was the first to look away. He made his way to the card room with young Dorset, leaving Carl to stare after him. They did not see each other for the rest of that night and when Andrew left the function with his guardian, he said, 'I saw Carl.'

'Who?'

'The new Lord Ashley.'

'Oh, yes. That chap. He's causing something of a sensation, I believe. He's so damned good looking everybody wants to meet him. I'm told he's quite a wit in the drawing rooms of London.'

'Old Lord Ashley was afraid the old tragedy would repeat itself,' said Andrew anxiously.

'Old Ashley was a villain socially and financially. He was also slightly mad. The fellow you call Carl is evidently making amends, from what I hear.'

'Nevertheless, his father did try to kill me.'

'So you say.'

'I was there, Eve,' Andrew protested, feeling at odds with his guardian over the significance of the family feud.

'In any event, dear boy, it wasn't Carl who tried to kill you. He would probably have been terribly upset by the whole affair.'

'I hadn't thought of that. Perhaps he personally doesn't mean me any harm.'

'Did you think he did?'

'Well ... Yes.'

'Forget it.'

Andrew said no more. Lord Evesham had dismissed the subject from his mind and there was no point in pursuing it. Andrew felt momentarily relieved, but the old fear returned. He could not accept his guardian's easy, flippant dismissal of what could result in a dreadful tragedy ending in his own death. He could not but help feeling that the family feud, was still very much alive, else why should his stomach turn over and feel like ice at the sight of Carl, whom he wanted to love? His fear stemmed from what Fate had in store for him more than from any manipulation on the part of a single member of the Ashley family.

Andrew did not see Carl again until one evening in his Club. Lord Drummond, his father, had been an indifferent card player, not caring if he played or not, but Andrew took it seriously. His many years of enforced loneliness had led him to find diversion in the manipulation of playing cards. The loss or gain of money was little to him compared with the losing or winning of the actual game. For that reason, probably, he was often successful.

On this occasion there were several other players in the room and a few loungers looking on at the games, quite a few round Andrew's table. Usually Andrew didn't take any notice of such onlookers, so immersed was he in the game. But on this occasion he was losing. Never had he known such bad luck. All the cards were against him, as if some evil influence were at work. After an hour, during a pause in the game and after having lost a good deal of money to young Dorset, he looked up and for the first time noticed the onlookers around him. Directly opposite to him, standing behind Dorset's chair and looking him full in the face, was Carl.

Andrew suddenly felt cold. All he could do was stare back at the man. Then he suddenly slapped his cards down on the table, pushed his chair back and strode out of the room. (He was told later that Carl took his place at the table and won a lot of money).

Next day Andrew found that the tittle-tattle of fools was adding to his discomfiture. The loungers round the table had seen him look up and stare at Carl, fling his cards down and leave the room. It was construed that he had affronted Carl in public. Even Lord Evesham had heard some of the gossip.

'London is a vast whispering gallery,' mused the old man.

'They know about you and Carl. Or think they do. They know about the duel between your two fathers.'

'Oh, well,' concluded Andrew. 'So long as it gives them something to talk about.'

Lord Evesham seemed unusually expansive.

'Relations between the Ashleys and the Drummonds have always been bad,' he ventured. 'Yet the two families have a strange affection for each other. Over the years they've even intermarried. Perhaps that's the problem.'

'Have you met him? Carl?' asked Andrew.

'I was introduced to him at the Dorsets'. He seemed a nice sort of fellow. It's a pity you have a grudge against him.'

'But I haven't!' Andrew protested vigorously.

'I'm glad to hear it,' said Lord Evesham. 'Because I've invited him to dinner.'

'You have?' cried Andrew in amazement.

'Yes,' said Lord Evesham blandly. 'I want to get to know him.'

'But...' Andrew began to protest.

'No buts, dear boy. It's time you met him on the accepted social terms.'

They had been talking in the library and suddenly Andrew decided not to stay to hear any more. He left the room and returned to his own quarters. Lord Evesham expected him to sit down to dinner with Carl. Andrew did not look forward to it and searched his brain for an excuse. Although he had nothing against Carl and was, in fact, fond of him, he was still frightened of him, actually frightened. He had almost affronted him in public, according to the rules of so-called society. He could not dispel from his mind the air of menace associated with Carl.

Andrew did not attend the dinner that his guardian had arranged. He played truant and dined instead with a friend at the Cafe Royal. It was a very pleasant meal in congenial company in spite of a niggling feeling at the back of his mind that kept telling him he was doing something wrong. This feeling was emphasised when at the end of the meal, a friend of his guest approached the table. The two were introduced and the friend said, rather pointedly, 'I'm surprised to see you here tonight, Drummond.'

'Oh,' said Andrew. 'Why?'

'My friend Lord Ashley said he was dining with you tonight at Lord Evesham's.'

'He told you wrong,' Andrew commented, abruptly.

'I thought there must be some mistake,' the man went on. 'He would scarcely be dining with you after you insulted him at the Club.' With that he went on his way.

'I didn't insult Ashley,' Andrew protested.

'Take no notice,' said his friend. 'That man's a dangerous gossip.'

'Seems like it.'

The friend, however, was curious. 'Was Ashley supposed to be dining with you tonight?'

'He's dining with my guardian,' said Andrew.

'He probably assumed you'd be there.'

'Probably.'

Again Andrew's conscience caused him to wonder if he'd done the right thing. It would seem that he hadn't. Carl, according to gossip, was expecting to meet him at the house, wanting to, evidently. Was that a gesture of friendliness? Could it be trusted? It would appear that Carl himself harboured no ill feeling following the incident at the Club. What would they say to each other if they met? Would they simply reminisce about the days at Ashley Castle, the time Carl accused Andrew of pushing him into the lake? Sitting on the stairs listening to the music? The time Carl's hand reached out for his? Is that what he was trying to do now, reach out a friendly hand?

There was only one word to describe Andrew's feelings as he left the restaurant – guilty.

He had an unpleasant exchange with his guardian when they were having breakfast together the next morning.

'Are you in the habit of insulting people, Andrew?' asked Lord Evesham quietly.

'No. I don't think so,' answered Andrew, not unaware of the tenor of his guardian's remark.

'You mean you don't know when you're doing it?'

'I mean I don't intend to.'

'That could still be because you can't help it.'

'Whom have I insulted?' asked Andrew.

'Me,' Lord Evesham told him.

'You?'

'Yes. Me.'

'How?'

'You were expected to dine with me last night.'

'I sent a message,' said Andrew lamely.

'At the last moment. I told you I'd invited Lord Ashley to dinner.'

'To get to know him, you said.'

'Exactly. With you.'

'Why with me?'

'Because you are part of this household. Or didn't you notice?'

'I already had a dinner engagement.'

'I don't believe you.'

'I can't help what you believe.'

'Don't be insolent.'

'I'm not.'

'You sent a message by your man Benson only late afternoon, asking young Evans to dine with you at the Cafe Royal. I don't call that a prior engagement.'

There was a somewhat militant silence between them.

'Well?' asked Lord Evesham, eventually.

Andrew hesitated before explaining, haltingly, 'I'm sorry. I'm nervous of meeting Carl again.'

Lord Evesham gave a little laugh. 'Did you think he was going to draw a pistol at the dining table?'

'No.'

'What then?'

'You know how I feel about him.'

'Yes. And you know what I said before. Misplaced, mistaken and stupid.'

'I'm frightened of him,' Andrew admitted, abruptly.

'Stupid,' cried Lord Evesham again.

'There's something cold about him,' Andrew went on, excitedly. 'He's never bothered about his sister, Eloise.'

'How can he?' stormed Lord Evesham. 'They were parted when they were children. He's been living abroad and you've buried his sister in a house by the river. Come to that, has Eloise bothered about her brother?'

'Well, no,' admitted Andrew. 'She never knew where he was.'

'She does now.'

'No. I don't think so. She'll only know when I tell her. She's out of touch with London.'

'Perhaps you would like to effect a meeting between them,' suggested Lord Evesham, with a touch of sarcasm.

'No, thank you. I don't mind dealing with Eloise. She's harmless. She's no believer in feuds. She doesn't even resent the fact that my father killed hers.'

'As far as you know,' put in Lord Evesham.

'What do you mean?' asked Andrew, fearfully.

'She's unlikely to harbour any resentment after all you've done for her. It's called expediency.'

'She's not like that.'

'No?'

'Nevertheless, Carl is a different cup of tea. Much as I want to like him, he wasn't slow to try to get me into trouble when we first met at Ashley Castle.'

'I must say he struck me as a man capable of great passion one way or another.'

'That's what I'm frightened of.'

'I've told you. Your fear is misplaced.'

'I don't think so.'

'Do you think he would have consented to dine here if he harboured any harm towards you?'

'His father managed to inveigle us into what he called a Reconciliation Ball, which turned out to be an elaborate trap.'

'You, of course,' conceded Lord Evesham, 'are the last of the Drummonds, so in ridding himself of you he would be ridding the Ashleys of the whole root of the feud. Is that what you think?'

'Something like that.'

'It's too fantastic to believe.'

'You mean only an Ashley could think of it.'

'I could believe it of Carl's father but not of the boy.'

'I don't want to take the risk,' admitted Andrew.

'That's up to you, of course. But don't make such a limp excuse the next time you don't want to dine with me.'

'I'm sorry about that. I must say I had a guilty conscience all the evening.'

'Serves you right,' declared Lord Evesham.

There was an uncomfortable silence between them again. Andrew was anxious to know what his guardian and Carl had talked about the night before.

'What did he have to say?' he asked eventually.

'Say!' burst out Lord Evesham. 'He said nothing. He looked sad and depressed. If he'd been a girl instead of a man, a girl in love with you, he could not have held himself with more restraint. All he muttered was, "I had hoped to meet someone else".'

'I'm told he is a girl,' said Andrew, simply.

Lord Evesham looked more shocked than puzzled.

'What did you say?' he asked.

'Because Lord Ashley was frightened that history might repeat itself, he insisted on his daughter being brought up as a boy.'

'Where did you learn that?'

'Eloise told me. When I was at the castle years ago.'

'She was having you on. A childish prank.'

'Benson told me as well.'

'Servants' gossip. Forget it.'

'I've never felt sure.'

'More fool you.'

'You won't say anything? I mean . . .'

'Do you take me for a fool like yourself? I wouldn't dream of spreading such an incredible tale. Not only would I feel ridiculous, I'd lay myself open to slander.'

'Now you can understand my feelings.'

'No. I can't. The feud between your two families is over

now that there are no members left to carry it on. Believe me.'

'The only members left are Carl and me, and we've been circling each other like fighting dogs since he came to London.'

'Have you spoken to him?'

'No. Of course not.'

Lord Evesham's wrath that he had displayed at the beginning of the conversation had by now evaporated into a normal, warm exchange, due no doubt to Andrew's explanation of his feelings. The insult, as far as Lord Evesham was concerned, was forgotten, if not forgiven. On the other hand, the insult inflicted upon Carl, occasioned by Andrew's absence from the dinner table, may not have been forgiven. Neither Andrew nor his guardian could know if Carl had gone away nursing a grievance determined upon some kind of revenge.

Andrew rode over to Riverside Towers to see Franz and Eloise. The rehearsals at Covent Garden for his opera *Ondine* had almost wrecked the poor man with their worry and anxiety. As for Eloise, in the few months since they had last met, she had changed subtly and wonderfully. Andrew had last seen the girl in a bridal gown. She was now a woman who had matured without gaining a wrinkle or losing a trace of the beauty of her youth. Marriage had ripened her. Her every movement was marked by that self-contained grace that her mother had had.

The first thing Andrew noticed as he walked onto the terrace was the return of the house martins nesting under the eaves. He always felt his heart lift when he saw them swooping across the sky, just as he always felt a pang of sadness when they left. There had been plenty of them at Drummond Castle but he never saw any in London.

Andrew told Eloise of his encounter with Carl and reminded Franz of the occasion when they were on the stairs at Ashley Castle. Franz remembered the incident with pleasure, but Eloise was worried about Carl's intentions. They had never been very close as children. Carl was always aloof and introspective, brooding. He sometimes frightened her. When Andrew told her that Carl seemed sad to have missed him at dinner she seemed somewhat pacified. But when Franz was out of earshot, Eloise reminded Andrew that Carl had been in a way responsible for the attempt on his life. She also reminded him that Carl was a girl. At that he laughed aloud.

'That's what you told me at the castle.'

'It's true.'

'It can't be. When I said that to my guardian he couldn't stop laughing.'

'You can laugh,' Eloise warned.

Becoming serious, Andrew asked, 'Have you ever seen Carl naked?'

'No. Of course not. We had separate nursemaids and separate bedrooms.

'There you are then.'

'But one of the servants told me.'

'I can't help being very fond of Carl. I always have been,' declared Andrew.

'That's history repeating itself,' said Eloise.

'I have no desire to murder Carl.'

'You don't know that Carl doesn't mean you harm.'

'Why?'

'Because it's inbred in the Ashleys. Father was obsessed by it.'

'I must say when I first saw your father at that hotel he frightened me.'

'Mother used to say he was wicked, but she could do nothing about it. And Carl is probably carrying on the tradition.'

'But you're not like that, Eloise.'

'No.'

'Neither was your mother.'

'No. It's the male side.'

'So Carl can't be a girl,' concluded Andrew.

'Beware of him, Andrew. That's all I say.'

'Don't worry, dear. I will.'

After a brief silence Andrew asked: 'Don't you want to meet him?'

'Carl?' mused Eloise. 'I'm afraid he might shatter my dreams.'

'You are now the wife of a famous composer.'

'And, as such, accepted by society,' said Eloise, pointedly.

'Yes,' agreed Andrew. 'Even my guardian confirms that.'

'Strange, isn't it?' commented Eloise. 'Until I married Franz I would have been rejected. Or, rather, until Franz became famous.'

'I never agreed with . . .' Andrew began.

'I know you didn't, dear,' Eloise comforted him. 'But you and I can have our little laugh at society, as it's called.'

'Yes,' said Andrew. 'And we will.'

The two grown-up children, for such they always seemed, parted affectionately.

Andrew's next meeting with Eloise and Franz was at the opening night of the opera. It was a glittering affair with everybody of any importance attending. Andrew asked Mr Dravenski what he thought of its chances of success.

'Assured,' said Mr Dravenski, tersely. 'Tastes and fashions may change, but this piece is quite indestructible.'

Andrew had never been more excited than he was that night. In spite of Mr Dravenski's assurance, he felt that the fate of his friend was in the balance. He was more nervous even than Franz himself, who seemed quite calm. He was to conduct the orchestra, of course.

Andrew arrived before the theatre was filled. It was half full and still filling up. He and Eloise took their places in Lord Evesham's box, situated in the first tier. Gradually box after box became a galaxy of stars. Diamonds, ribbons and orders reflected the brilliant light which flooded the house. Fans fluttered like gorgeous butterflies and the whole house became a scene of splendour filled with the perfume of flowers. Andrew's heart leapt as he compared this scene with the night he had met Franz at the Students' Ball. Then he had been an unknown composer with a threadbare coat, but now he was drawing all the wealth and beauty of London to his opera. There was an electrical feeling in the theatre, a feeling that Andrew could not describe until Lord Evesham said, 'Success is in the air, I think, Andrew.'

And then, from the orchestra came the first complaints of the violin strings and the deep grunting of the cellos as the musicians tuned their instruments. And there was Franz in complete evening attire. Andrew's mind went back once again to the staircase at Ashley Castle, when he had been with Eloise and Carl, peering through the banisters at the musicians below.

The taps of Franz's baton brought forth the first bars from the orchestra. Andrew sat holding Eloise's hand as he listened. They both recognised the little tune that he had played to them under the oak tree at Riverside Towers.

When the curtain fell on the first act the opera was already a success.

'Ah, yes!' sighed Lord Evesham. 'That is music. Beside it, Wagner sounds like a hurdy-gurdy.' He then left the box to talk to his friends in their own boxes. Andrew was left with Eloise.

'It's a success already,' he told her.

'Dear Franz,' she murmured. 'It means so much to him.'

There was a knock on the door of the box. Andrew left Eloise leaning over the balcony to watch the glittering throng as he got up to open the door. He was confronted by Carl. They stood looking at each other. Then Andrew noticed that Carl had two friends with him, friends unknown to Andrew.

'Lord Drummond,' said Carl, 'I have a compliment to pay you.'

Andrew was expecting some pleasant expression and thought briefly to ask him in to meet his sister, but suddenly the white glove in Carl's hand flicked him on the shoulder. Once again they stood just looking at each other. Then Andrew bowed in acknowledgement of the challenge. Carl turned and left with his two friends.

Eloise had neither heard nor seen what happened. It was a deadly insult very nicely wrapped up in the word 'compliment'.

So it was to be. It seemed that the confrontation was bound to come. Carl had challenged him now and Andrew could not escape. Andrew was not without a certain amount of animal courage inherited from his father, and yet the thought occurred to him immediately of leaving London and ignoring the studied insult. He would sacrifice name and honour rather than submit to his Fate. Some instinct told him that the inevitable duel would have consequences far beyond what he could imagine, that it would be a turning point in his life. He did not doubt the outcome of the duel, as he had never doubted the outcome of the duel between their fathers. He would not kill Carl, he would only wound him slightly. He loved him too much to kill him. When he returned to his seat Eloise turned away from the balcony.

'Who was that?' she asked, casually.

'Carl.'

'Carl?' Eloise echoed in surprise. 'Didn't he want to see me? Where is he?'

She made for the door to chase after her brother, but Andrew put a hand out to restrain her and led her back to her seat. Her slight exasperation was stilled when Andrew said, 'He came to challenge me to a duel.'

'Andrew!' she cried in horror. 'You can't!'

Neither of them said anything for a horrified moment.

'What are you going to do?' asked Eloise, quietly.

'I'll send him my seconds in the morning, of course.'

'Why don't you go away?' Eloise suggested, fearfully.

'I can't do that.'

At that moment Lord Evesham returned to the box and having heard the last remark asked casually, 'What can't you do?'

Eloise explained excitedly what had happened in the old man's absence.

'I just passed the fellow in the corridor,' said Lord Evesham. 'I thought he looked rather pleased with himself.'

They were not able to discuss the matter further as the curtain rose on the second act of the opera. Andrew wanted Eloise to enjoy the success of the evening so he squeezed her hand as they sat together. But he and Carl had an account to settle and that was that.

105

The opera was a great success. The audience cheered it to the roof of the building. Franz took so many bows that his back ached, and the audience laughed when he put his hand to his back in mock agony. Some of the ladies from other boxes burst into Lord Evesham's to make a fuss of Eloise as the wife of the composer, simply to be able to say that they knew her. Lord Evesham was not slow to notice the antics of those who would otherwise have spurned the girl. The success was dimmed for Andrew though, as he seemed to view everything now as if from a distance.

At supper that night Eloise wanted to call on her brother to try to persuade him to call off the challenge, but both Andrew and Lord Evesham forbade her to make any contact with the man. It was against all the rules, and in spite of the girl's vehement protests, the rules were adhered to.

Poor Franz, who could not bear quarrels of any kind and would not hurt a fly, sat silent, letting the arguments range about him. He couldn't help feeling that the challenge cast a shadow over his success, particularly as it involved his beloved benefactor.

Andrew chose as his seconds Lord Dorset and Lord Evesham, who offered himself. Lord Dorset was commissioned to take the counter-challenge to Lord Ashley. He returned with the news that the counter-challenge had been accepted but with an extraordinary proviso: the duel was not to take place until three months hence.

'He will fight you today if you insist,' said Lord Dorset. 'But he asked me to tell you that he would require three months in order to arrange his affairs.'

'Very well,' said Andrew. 'I accept.'

'I consider the delay an insult in itself,' complained Lord Dorset.

'No,' said Andrew, dreamily. 'It's like him. He's a strange man.'

'I don't care for him very much,' added Lord Dorset.

'Don't you?' Andrew said and laughed.

'I don't understand why he should challenge you in the

first place,' Lord Dorset insisted. 'You haven't insulted him in any way.'

'He thinks I have.'

'It seems a very forced business to me. I don't like the smell of it,' Lord Dorset scoffed.

'There have been several duels to the death between our families,' Andrew explained. 'He obviously wants them to continue. The feud has been going on for over a hundred years. We will meet in three months' time.'

Lord Dorset felt far from happy with the new arrangement and said so.

When Andrew told his guardian of the new arrangement, he was as perplexed as Lord Dorset.

'I was rather pleased about the duel at first,' he said. 'You are a good swordsman. Like your father. And it's good for a young man to prove himself. But three months! Forty-eight hours should be enough time for a man to put his house in order. What business can he possibly have that requires three months' attention? I don't like the sound of it.'

'It's a long time, I admit,' conceded Andrew. 'But I have to accept the condition.'

'The Ashleys always were an odd lot,' concluded Lord Evesham.

Andrew made up his mind that Death now stared him in the face. Swords were the weapons chosen by Carl, so it must be assumed that he fancied himself as a swordsman. Andrew was an expert himself, but he was determined not to pierce Carl. The old fatality that had attended the relationship between the Ashleys and the Drummonds would come to an end. He was condemned to fight, not to kill. And he was prepared to be Carl's victim if necessary. All through the summer the thought filled him with a vague melancholy, a mist that made the landscape of life more beautiful, its distances and its beauties more grand, its trivialities more futile. Only when we come to the end do we see life as it is and things in their proper proportions. Andrew had seen the splendour of Society in all its glory. He didn't think that he would regret leaving it. It never entered into his consideration. It was nothing to him, nothing beside the appeal of spring and summer, the cry of life that comes from all things bright and all things fair, from flowers, from birds, from the heart.

Andrew spent a lot of time at Riverside Towers during those anxious months. He enjoyed the company of Eloise and Franz. They often picnicked by the river and the jetty that still hadn't been repaired.

The day before the duel, the fourth of July, Andrew called on his second, Lord Dorset, to discuss the arrangements for the following day.

'Ah!' cried Dorset in greeting. 'I'm glad to see you, Drummond.'

'Oh?' said Andrew, for the other man's manner indicated something more than an ordinary greeting.

'I heard last night that you had come to an amicable understanding with Ashley.'

'Understanding?'

'People say you've apologised to him.'

'Apologised? How can I? It was he who insulted me. He struck me with his glove. That is the traditional insult, as you know. So how can I apologise?'

'Then it's a false rumour?'

'It certainly is. I will meet Lord Ashley at seven o'clock tomorrow morning as arranged.'

'Very well. Till then.'

'Till then.'

Andrew took his leave feeling puzzled. As Lord Evesham remarked, there was something not straightforward about this duel. First the delay, now the rumour about reconciliation.

That night Andrew said to Benson, 'Don't forget to call me at five o'clock.'

'I won't forget, my lord. If only I could.' Benson looked sad. He had grown old, of course, as he had served Andrew all the years before and since his father's death.

'I don't like it,' he said, glumly.

'I know you don't, Benson. Neither do I. But it has to be done.'

'Those Ashleys,' Benson muttered.

Andrew slept well, much to his surprise. He actually felt glad that he was meeting Carl again. Perhaps after the duel they could be friends. That is, if Carl didn't kill him. Andrew had no idea of the quality of Carl's swordsmanship. He couldn't help feeling that the whole idea of the duel was more of a gesture than a challenge, as Lord Evesham suspected. It didn't have the wilful intent, for instance, that epitomised the one between their fathers when Carl's father was killed.

'Five o'clock,' intoned Benson.

'It's all right. I'm awake,' said Andrew.

Benson was standing by the window with a bath towel over his arm. He had drawn the curtains and the light of early morning filled the room. Andrew dressed quickly and had his breakfast. He felt both nervous and excited. Then he sat down and wrote a letter to Eloise and Franz. In case of his death, he divided his property leaving half to Eloise and half to Franz. When he had finished the letter, Benson appeared again.

'The carriage is at the door,' he said.

Andrew sealed the letter and handed it to Benson. 'In case of an accident,' he said.

Benson took the letter and put it in his pocket without looking at the inscription. He was grave. He had known and looked after Andrew since he was born, and an affinity had developed between them. But this morning was different. This morning Benson was the servant and Andrew the master.

As Andrew stepped from the front door to the pavement, he felt that he was stepping into another world, a man's world. Everything had been a lovely game until now. This morning the grim business of life had begun.

Benson got up on the box and they set off. Lord Evesham would follow in his own carriage.

The sun was bright on the trees, which were waving in the early morning breeze. A bird was singing. Everything was beautiful. It seemed a pity to have to die on a morning like this, to shut one's eyes forever and never see the sun again or hear a bird sing. As they drew near their destination, Andrew felt as he had often felt on leaving home as a child. He had a strong desire to return. On this occasion he daren't, of course.

The chosen venue for the duel was a lovely place, sheltered by trees, on a hill overlooking the whole of London. It was a favourite spot for settling affairs of honour.

'We are first,' said Benson, turning round.

Andrew alighted and stood outside the carriage. There was no other carriage in sight. They were, in fact, ten minutes before their time, which was a great mistake; for ten minutes of waiting in an affair of this description was very unsettling for the nerves. Andrew paced up and down, for the early morning air was chilly on the hill. It promised to be a lovely day. How much of it would Andrew see?

Andrew heard the sound of carriage wheels on gravel. A carriage was being driven rapidly along the lane towards the clearing. There were three gentlemen in it, Carl's seconds and the obligatory surgeon. Then Andrew's seconds arrived, Lord Evesham and Lord Dorset.

The seconds of each party bowed to each other. Someone took out his watch. Then someone else did. They compared the time. There was obviously some delay.

'By the way,' said Lord Dorset, 'has anyone seen anything of Lord Ashley during the last three months?'

'I haven't,' said one.

'Neither have I,' said another.

'Let's hope he turns up,' said Lord Evesham.

'He's late anyway,' concluded Lord Dorset.

Andrew looked at his watch. It was now ten minutes past seven, an inexcusable delay on Carl's part, a gross display of bad manners considering the circumstances. Unless, of course an accident had occurred.

Five more minutes slowly passed. The gentleman with the mahogany box under his arm that contained the surgical instruments began to pace up and down. The sun struck the hilts of the rapiers which one of the seconds was carrying concealed in the folds of his dark blue overcoat.

'At twenty minutes past,' said Lord Dorset, 'I shall declare the duel postponed. I shall take my principal home and I shall demand an explanation and an apology from Lord Ashley.'

He had scarcely uttered the words when the surgeon declared, 'Here he comes!'

A closed carriage drawn by two magnificent black horses was advancing at a furious pace. Andrew could not have given any reason, but he got the impression that it was a funeral carriage, what with the closed windows and the black horses. At the same time the sun went in. The carriage came to a halt only a few paces from Andrew and his seconds. The carriage door opened and a lady stepped out. She was an exquisite apparition of no more than twenty years of age. The sight of her was so unexpected that the men around Andrew, used as they were to beauty, world weary and cynical, remained motionless as statues, mouths agape. Andrew smiled to himself.

The girl, of course, was Carl, the real Carl, Carl the girl. Andrew again heard the voice of Eloise telling him that Carl was a girl. The beautiful lady now stood surveying the gathering.

'I have come on behalf of Lord Ashley,' she announced. 'I regret to tell you that he died abroad last night.'

There was an audible gasp among the men standing around her. Lord Dorset clutched at Andrew's sleeve.

'That's odd,' he whispered. 'I could have sworn that this was Lord Ashley himself. She's like him, too. Must be his sister.'

'It's not his sister,' said Andrew.

'On Lord Ashley's behalf,' Carl went on, 'I apologise to Lord Drummond.'

Carl turned to Andrew with her lips half parted in a glad smile. Their eyes met and Andrew felt that he was happy for the first time in his life. He found himself holding again the soft hands that he had not felt for so many years.

Slowly he became aware of his surroundings. He said goodbye to his seconds and escorted Carl to his own carriage where Benson was waiting dutifully. Carl put her arm through Andrew's and hugged it. Benson climbed up onto the box and they drove away, leaving the rest of the company somewhat bewildered.

Sitting in the carriage as closely together as they could get, Carl said, 'Do you remember, Andrew, when you pushed me into the lake?'

Andrew chuckled and held the girl closer to him. 'I didn't push you, Carl, and you know it,' he said.

'Don't you think you should call me Carla?' she suggested.

'I would rather call you beloved.'

'That, too.'

Silently they enjoyed their own company for a moment, holding hands and loving each other as if they had always been together. Carla closed her eyes in ecstasy. Then, as if waking from a dream, she asked, 'Where are we going?'

'Home. Where you belong. I want to hold you and kiss you to death.'

'A lovely death,' she murmured.

When they arrived at the house, Benson opened the door of the carriage. Once Andrew had alighted, he helped Carla to descend and they both made their way into the house.

As soon as they were in Andrew's drawing room they stood in a passionate embrace, lips and mouths devouring each other, bodies slumped together in abandon. Inevitably they lost their balance and fell onto the sofa, still clutching each other.

'God, I love you, Carla,' murmured Andrew.

It was not long before they were both half undressed and caressing each other's warm flesh. After the first flush of physical pleasure they slumped beside each other on the sofa, breathless and dishevelled. As they began to adjust their clothing Carla said, 'You know, that time you left the castle I nearly died. I'd fallen in love with you even then.'

'And I with you. Even though you were a boy.'

'Father kept telling me to beware of you all the time you were there. He wanted me to kill you.'

'You?'

'Yes.'

'How? We were only children.'

'He wanted me to suffocate you in bed while you were asleep. I said I couldn't.'

'So he tried to do it instead.'

'Yes.'

'And nearly succeeded.'

'I'm glad he didn't.'

'So am I,' agreed Andrew, sitting decorously beside Carla now on the sofa. 'Or I wouldn't be sitting beside you like this, loving the very presence of you. By the way, dear, aren't you hungry? It was cold out there.'

'A little,' she admitted.

Andrew rang for Benson and arranged for breakfast and coffee to be served. The lovers chatted away while they ate and drank, just as though they'd been doing it all their lives, such was the affinity between them.

'Mother accused Father of arranging the Reconciliation Ball as a trick to get you there,' declared Carla.

'That's what my guardian thought. He wouldn't believe that you were a girl, though.'

'Did you know? I thought it was a well kept secret.'

'There was a lot of gossip.'

'He should have known when I nearly choked on that cigar of his at dinner.'

They both laughed.

'I cursed you that night, Andrew. You were supposed to be there.'

'I was frightened.'

'Of me?'

'Yes.'

'Silly boy.'

Strange, he thought, how that expression made him feel wanted.

'I found it difficult sometimes trying to be a man,' explained Carla. 'Being a boy wasn't so difficult. When Father was away, Mother dressed me as a girl, but I wasn't allowed to meet anyone, not even Eloise, in case they told Father, and Mother would then suffer. Everyone was fright-

113

ened of Father because he had this terrible obsession about history repeating itself. She could only make me a girl surreptitiously. It was funny.'

'And here we are repeating history,' Andrew reminded her.

'Yes. Poor Father would be horrified.'

'He needn't be. I wouldn't hurt you for the world. I love you too much.'

'So did those others, the honeymoon couple, the ones who started all the trouble.'

'Don't talk about them,' urged Andrew. 'Let them rest in peace. We have our own lives to live. Together, I hope.'

Carla reached out and took his hand, just as she had done on the stairs all those years ago. She didn't need to say anything. They both understood.

'Let's go and walk in the garden,' suggested Andrew. 'There's a lake. So be careful.'

Carla laughed as he led her out of the room.

On the way downstairs they met Lord Evesham.

'What the devil's going on?' demanded his lordship.

'Eve,' said Andrew calmly, 'this is Carla who used to be Carl, Lord Ashley.'

'My God, woman,' exclaimed Eve, 'you're beautiful.'

'Thank you,' said Carla.

'Where are you off to now, Andrew, having got us all up at the crack of dawn?'

'I'm going to show Carla the garden.'

'Off you go then. I'll catch up with you later.'

He stood aside to let the loving couple pass arm in arm. He turned to watch them, thoroughly approving of the spectacle.

As they strolled arm in arm in the beautiful garden, Carla said, 'Do you know, Andrew, as a man I found myself pursued by the ladies.'

'I'm not surprised,' declared Andrew.

'I came to London to find you, you know. But you avoided me.'

'I've told you why.'

'The only way I could force you to meet me was by challenging you to a duel.'

'I'd made up my mind not to hurt you.'

'Oh, I'm not a bad swordsman. Father taught me. Part of his plan.'

'Tell me, dear,' said Andrew. 'Why did you insist on a three month delay?'

'I had to let my hair grow,' she laughed. 'And get rid of those restricting bandages I had to wear round my chest.'

'I see. No ill effects, I noticed.'

'No,' admitted Carla.

'You're such a lovely colour, Carla. Olive. Beautiful.'

'Thank you.'

As they reached the lake and stood looking into the water and watching the ducks and moorhens, Andrew hugged Carla's arm to him, enjoying the aroma of the woman he loved.

'Oh, Carla. We must never part again. We've wasted so much time.'

'No,' she replied. 'I am yours now. Carl is dead. Only Carla remains. There's no one to trouble us now.'

They made their way back to the house.

'You remember your sister, Eloise?' said Andrew.

'Yes,' replied Carla. 'She was in the box with you at the opera, wasn't she?'

'Yes. Why don't we go and see her? I'm sure she'd love to meet you again.'

'Where is she?'

'She lives in a house that I have by the river.'

'Your house?'

'Yes.'

'I see.'

Carla was strangely silent after that enigmatic remark and her silence puzzled Andrew. It was so long since Carla had met her sister that perhaps she was wondering how she would be greeted. So thought Andrew, naively.

'I met her by accident at a students' ball,' Andrew went on. 'She was living in a veritable hovel after your mother died.

She, poor soul, was almost begging, I believe. I rescued Eloise and set her up in this house by the river. We could drive down there to lunch. What do you say?'

'Yes. Of course,' answered Carla, quietly.

With Benson once again on the box of the carriage, they drove down to Riverside Towers at a leisurely pace, sitting close together, cocooned in their new found intimacy. Andrew did not notice Carla's silence enough to be worried about it. He was simply content to be with her.

The slowing of the carriage as they arrived at their destination threw the lovers apart. Andrew helped Carla down from the carriage and led her by the hand to the front door, which was opened by Hawley. Andrew led the way excitedly through the house to the terrace.

'Come on, Carla,' he urged as he hurried on ahead.

He saw Eloise sitting on her own in a big wicker chair on the terrace.

'Eloise!' he called. 'I've found little Carl!'

Eloise got up from her chair to meet him.

'Andrew! What is it?' she cried, in alarm.

'Little Carl is now Carla,' he explained, breathlessly. 'I've brought her to see you.'

Andrew reached out and took Eloise in an enthusiastic embrace, kissing her on both cheeks.

'Where is she?' Eloise asked, puzzled.

Andrew turned, laughing, to introduce Carla. She was not there.

'She's hiding,' he said, as he ran back into the house calling. 'Carla! Carla!'

He had assumed that she was following him as he made his eager way to the terrace. He retraced his steps, calling her name, back to the front door which was open. He went outside. The carriage had gone.

'Carla,' he called again, quietly, fearfully, as Eloise came to join him.

Andrew was suddenly frightened. What had happened? Where had Carla gone? And why? She had obviously gone off in the carriage with Benson.

'Where is she?' asked Eloise.

'She's gone off in the carriage,' said Andrew.

'Why?'

'I don't know,' declared Andrew, irritably, anxiously. 'I must go after her.'

'How?' asked Eloise. 'Franz went to London in our carriage.'

'I'll find one,' cried Andrew.

'Andrew!' Eloise called out.

But Andrew was already hurrying away. What could have frightened her away, he wondered as he strode along. Was she frightened of meeting Eloise? He had embraced Eloise as he told her that Carla was with him. Was that the reason? Was she jealous? Did she imagine that Eloise was his mistress, that there was something between them other than their platonic friendship? It was unbelievable. Was she angry about something? Should he have left her side to run to Eloise? To leave without an explanation! Why did Benson not wait? What urgency had prompted him to agree to her wishes? Andrew almost sobbed as he remembered how he had held her warm body to his, how they had kissed, tender, understanding kisses.

It took Andrew a long time to arrive at the house in London and when he did he rushed in as soon as the door was opened and shouted for Benson.

The agitated sound brought Lord Evesham from his study.

'What's going on?' he asked.

Andrew was about to run up the stairs but paused briefly to explain, breathlessly, 'I've lost her! I've lost Carla!'

'Where did you go with her?' complained Lord Evesham, calmly.

'I took her to Riverside Towers to meet Eloise, but before I could introduce them she'd vanished.'

'Like her father. Mad,' concluded Lord Evesham as he returned to his study.

Andrew ran up the stairs, Benson met him on the landing.

'Where did you take her?' Andrew demanded.

'To her house,' replied Benson.

'Why didn't you wait for me?'

'The lady was not to be refused. She was in tears.'

'Crying?' repeated Andrew, puzzled.

'What else do you call it?'

Benson, who not so long ago had considered any contact with the Ashley family fatal was now silently admonishing Andrew for his treatment of Carla Ashley, virtually accusing him of neglecting her.

Without another word Andrew turned and ran out of the house. He almost ran to the Ashley house. When he got there he found it empty and for sale. Where could she have gone? Andrew hurried on to Lord Dorset's house. He told his friend the whole story, including the boy-girl transformation. When Lord Dorset had recovered from the shock, he admitted that he did not know any of Carla's friends but suggested calling on the seconds. He gave their addresses to Andrew, who called on each in turn. They knew nothing of her whereabouts. The only address they had was the one she had left. Andrew might as well be searching for a ghost. But he was determined to find her even if it meant combing the whole of London.

Andrew returned weary and footsore to his quarters, where he was visited by his guardian.

'Benson told me what happened,' Eve said as he settled in one of the armchairs.

'I don't know why she ran away,' moaned Andrew.

'As I told you, dear boy, all the Ashleys are a little mad.'

'Carla's not mad.'

'Where were you when she ran away?'

'I was with Eloise.'

'Ah!' exclaimed Lord Evesham.

'What does that mean?'

'She's jealous.'

'What? How can she be?'

'That, of course, applied to a lady, is the most stupid question you could ask.'

'But how could she be jealous?' Andrew insisted.

'Did she meet Eloise?'

'No.'

'Why not?'

'I ran forward to tell Eloise that...'

'Leaving Carla behind?'

'Only a few yards.'

'And when you turned round she'd gone.'

'Yes.'

'How did you greet Eloise?'

'What do you mean, how did I greet Eloise?'

'Did you kiss her?'

'No.' Andrew corrected himself. 'Well, not exactly,' he explained.

'How exactly?' pursued Lord Evesham.

'In my excitement I hugged her and kissed her on each cheek. That's all.'

'That, my naive one, is where you went wrong,' declared Lord Evesham.

'How?'

'Need you ask?'

'So I'm to blame?'

Lord Evesham merely shrugged his shoulders.

In his unworldly way it seemed that Andrew had driven his loved one away. After all that they had said to each other, how could she have doubted his feelings for her? Eloise was merely a childhood friend, not even a childhood sweetheart, whereas he and Carla were fated to be affinities, to be lovers.

From now on Andrew almost lived on the streets. He visited every hotel within a wide radius and intended to extend his search. It became an obsession and he appeared frantic in his desperation. His friends either avoided him or tried to humour him. He wandered the streets, always on the lookout for his Carla. It was impossible to tell where she might be hiding. Ashley Castle? It no longer belonged to the Ashley family since the father's downfall.

Andrew dreaded the nights. He could not search at night because of the dark streets. Dear old Benson helped him in his search with never a word of reproach, faithful servant that he was.

119

Andrew caught sight of himself in a mirror and recognised the change. Haggard, white and drawn, he no longer had the face of a young man. But who could he turn to? There is generally among one's friends some person, some homely individual, some good man or good woman to whom one can turn in affliction for a word of consolation, or even just to feel their presence. Andrew could not think of anyone except Eloise, and in the circumstances, following Lord Evesham's assessment, he decided against such a move. Yet she was the only one he could talk to about Carla, for they both knew and, they thought, understood her.

As he left the house one morning to lunch with Lord Dorset, he told Benson that he would probably be driving down to Riverside Towers after lunch.

Lord Dorset had always been sympathetic and concerned for Andrew, not being possessed of the cynical attitude of the sophisticated Lord Evesham. Lord Dorset advised Andrew to be patient and to cease his searching. Carla was bound to appear somewhere sooner or later. For one thing she was too attractive not to be noticed, and there would no doubt be some official decision taken about the Ashley title. Lord Ashley was Lord Ashley when he had no right to be, because he was a girl. Carla couldn't go back to being Lord Ashley because she had said he was dead. Yet there was no funeral, no body. Could she call herself Lady Ashley? And where would Eloise fit in? All that could not be sorted out with someone in hiding. And nobody could hide forever.

Andrew felt somewhat comforted by Lord Dorset's words and instead of driving to Riverside Towers, he decided to return home and rest. He felt desperately tired. He might drive down to see Eloise tomorrow.

Benson met him at the front door. He seemed agitated.

'She's been here,' he gasped.

'Who?'

Andrew was almost too tired to speak.

'The one you've been looking for.'

Andrew's lethargy left him suddenly and he was alert.

'Where is she?'

He made to hurry into the house but Benson said, 'I told her you'd gone to Riverside Towers. You said . . .'

'Yes. Yes,' Andrew cut him short. 'Get the carriage. Quickly. You must drive me. Quickly, Benson.

Benson hurried away while Andrew paced up and down the street in front of the house. Carla had called while he was lunching with Lord Dorset and talking about her. Andrew had walked slowly home, still hoping to find her but not holding out much hope. And now . . .

The carriage arrived at the door with Benson on the box.

'Stay there!' Andrew commanded as Benson attempted to get down. He didn't want to waste time being helped into the carriage.

'Drive like the wind!' Andrew shouted.

And they were off. Several times during the journey Andrew was tempted to lower the window and urge Benson to go faster, but he could not risk the horses going lame. They had settled into a good swinging gait. All Andrew could do was sit back as patiently as possible and listen to the rumble of the carriage wheels and the beat of the horses' hooves on the road. There will be a carriage outside Riverside Towers, he imagined. That is, if Carla had indeed made the journey, which he hoped to God she had. If Benson had told her that he'd gone to Riverside Towers, surely she would make for there. What if he was wrong? In the end he could not resist. He pulled down the window and called up to Benson, 'Faster, Benson! Faster!'

'Yes. Yes. All right,' Benson answered and Andrew heard the crack of the whip.

At last they arrived at Riverside Towers. Andrew recognised the carriage with the two black horses. The same carriage and the same horses that had attended the duel.

Andrew got out of the carriage and hurried to the front door. He banged the knocker relentlessly. As soon as Hawley opened the door he pushed past him into the hall, calling out, 'Carla! Carla! Where are you?'

Eloise came out of the drawing room. Before she could say anything Andrew demanded, 'Where is she?'

'She went down to the river to wait for you,' replied Eloise.

Andrew did not hesitate. He ran through the house, across the terrace and down the lawn to the river.

'Carla! Carla!' he called as he ran.

He pulled up short at the river bank, breathless.

'Carla?'

Looking about he noticed that part of the balustrading surrounding the jetty had broken away. His stomach turned over. He ran onto the jetty.

'Carla!' he screamed.

He looked down into the water and there she was, floating face down, her long hair floating around her.

'Carla!' he screamed again.

He knelt down and grabbed hold of her. He hauled her out of the water onto the wooden staging. He called out to the house: 'Help! Help!'

He applied what artificial resuscitation he could but there was no reaction. Carla did not move or breathe. He looked up to see Eloise and Franz running down the lawn towards him.

'What's happened?' cried Eloise.

Franz knelt down and touched the side of Carla's neck. He looked up and shook his head. Carla was dead.

Andrew fell across her wet body and sobbed his heart out.